RESISTING MADNESS

WESLEY SOUTHARD

Resisting Madness

Copyright © 2019 by Wesley Southard

ISBN 978-1-950259-17-5

Cover Art by Justin T. Coons

For Mike Lombardo
You help make Pennsylvania tolerable.

For Paul,

Can you resist?

ACKNOWLEDGMENTS

Thank you to the following editors for publishing my short fiction in years past: Jessy Marie Roberts; Brian Keene; Christopher Jones, Nanci Kalanta, and Tony Tremblay; Herika R. Raymer and Terrie Leigh Relf; Adam Millard; Jacob Haddon; and CJ Miles IV.

Also, thank you to the following people for various reasons: Kelli Owen, Bob Ford, Mary SanGiovanni, Somer and Jessie Canon, Mike Lombardo, Stephen Kozeniewski, John Boden, Chris Enterline, Wile E. Young, Kyle Lybeck, the whole No*Con crew, Mom and Dad and Sis, Joe Ripple and the Scares That Care charity, Kevin Foster, and to many others I'm forgetting right now (sorry, my memory isn't great).

A massive thank you to Jarod Barbee and Patrick C. Harrison III for taking a chance on me and this collection. You guys rock!

And, as always, thank you to my lovely wife Katie. My rock.

TABLE OF CONTENTS

WITH MANY THANKS TO NEWARK

There was no way in hell he was going to make it.

The moment Tesh stepped off the plane, his few minutes in Hartsfield-Jackson International instantly became a marathon. He pushed through the crowded gate and made a beeline for the departure monitor, expecting the worst. He got it. With his next gate set at the opposite end of the terminal, he doubted if he'd even have time to see his flight take off without him. But he ran, red-faced and breathless, wanting to scream in frustration, nothing ever going his way—

Which made the ticket agent's smile that much worse.

The moment Tesh rounded the corner toward his gate, the man's grin leapt out like a flashlight in a dark room. Though few travelers still haunted the area, milling about like restless spirits, the agent's haughty, shit-eating grin immediately grabbed Tesh's attention. *Fucking creep*, he thought. *Only a TSA employee could wear such a carefree smirk, while the rest of us get to panic.*

"Stop!" Tesh screamed. "Hold the plane!" His body ached as he closed the gap between them.

The agent, still grinning, slowly shook his head.

"Please wait!"

Tesh nearly collided with the counter, covering the tremendous distance in a matter of seconds. His breaths were quick and harsh, his chest burning. At thirty-nine, he was not the young man he used to be.

"Christ!" Tesh gasped. He dropped his bag to the floor. "I'm sorry…I know I'm, like, twelve minutes late…but has the plane taken off yet?"

"No, sir, Mr. Hagman," said the agent. His name tag read: Frank. "You made it. We've been waiting for you."

"I'm really sorry. My plane…my plane from Newark didn't land until about two minutes ago…and I had to run like a bat out of Hell to get here. Goddamn snowstorm nearly screwed everything up!"

"We understand," the agent nodded, still smiling. "These things happen."

Tesh breathed deep and closed his eyes, fighting the urge to collapse. Considering he had only slept for three hours in the last two days, the floor looked awfully tempting.

"Mr. Hagman? They're waiting."

Tesh handed the agent his ticket to be scanned, then grabbed his bag and dashed into the boarding tunnel. "Thank you!"

The ticket agent sighed. "No…thank you."

The tunnel didn't lead directly into the plane as he'd hoped, instead coming out onto the tarmac itself, where the frosty night attacked him head-on. He shivered beneath his leather jacket, and pulled his bag higher over his shoulder.

In the darkness ahead, the express jet growled to life. The moment his eyes found the plane Tesh froze, and fought the urge to turn and run. His heart pounded, stomach turning corkscrews. It wasn't until now, as he faced the plane, that he finally understood what he was here for--where he was going. This was it: the last step in closing the gap.

Please hurry, son. I need you.

An icy blast of wind licked his face, snapping him out of his daze. With his father's words fading, he began climbing the steps leading into the plane. Midway up he stopped, suddenly wondering, *How did the ticket agent know my name?* Tesh glanced over his shoulder.

In the overhead window, the ticket agent stood alone, staring down at him. The man nodded once, then turned and disappeared.

***

Snow began to fall as Tesh stepped into the warm cabin of the plane. His head held low, he slipped past a pair of smiling stewardesses and hobbled down the first few rows, ignoring the random grumbles at his tardiness.

Shove it up your ass, he thought.

As he stepped into economy class—because it's all his father could afford—he immediately noticed the two men sitting in the front row to his left. He couldn't help but stare. The young man in the aisle seat, roughly in his early twenties, was curled up tight, muttering to himself. He trembled fiercely, like a car with a bent axle, and was as white as a sheet of paper. His long blond hair hung over his face as he rocked back and forth. In the adjoining window seat, an older man with slicked-back black hair and a thick mustache seemed quite the opposite as he slept peacefully, unbothered by his neighbor's ill jitters. A large grin was stretched across his lips.

What the hell is with everyone smiling today? Surely Tesh wasn't the only one with a dying father?

Directly behind them, Tesh found his seat in 2B. He frowned.

At first glance, Tesh immediately didn't like his neighbor. Already a cramped space, the man's respectable girth spilled over into Tesh's seat, making him want to stomp and scream. The man reeked of whiskey and chatted loudly into his cell phone, as if he were the only person on the plane. Tesh balled his fists.

The man closed his phone then turned to Tesh. "Take a seat, hoss."

Tesh stuffed his bag into the overhead compartment, then squeezed into his half-filled seat, brushing against the man's damp shirt.

The man eyed the snow collecting on the window. "Fifty-five and sunny? Yeah, maybe in Hell. Meteorologists don't know shit about shit. Didn't see this massive snowstorm coming to gobble up the entire eastern seaboard. Yeah—more like didn't bother to tell us." He hiccupped. "So where you from?"

Tesh winced at his sour breath. "Newark."

"Jersey, eh? You got your own TV show, too? Seems like everybody's got a show in that state. Bunch of shit, if you ask me."

Ignoring his neighbor's casual profanity, Tesh watched the two stewardesses as they ran through the safety demonstration. The one closer to him, a short-haired blond with wide-set hips, grinned helpfully as she presented the oxygen masks and established all emergency exits. The one in business class, an older Asian woman, looked tired and uncomfortable as she ran through the motions. Once they finished, the blond approached her coworker and whispered into her ear. The older woman nodded and rubbed her stomach. They turned and headed toward the front of the cabin.

Tesh wasn't sure why, but the blond looked strangely familiar.

The overhead speakers squawked. *"Good evening, ladies and gentlemen, and welcome aboard flight 2110, traveling from Atlanta to Orlando. I am Captain Johnston, and I'll be accompanied by my trainee, Captain Abell. Tonight we will be traveling at an altitude of nearly twenty-five thousand feet, with a travel time of about two hours, maybe a little more, and very little chance of escape. Due to the unforeseen weather conditions, we may experience some slight turbulence, but no worries; we'll get you there in time. We'll be taking off momentarily, so just sit back and relax. Dinner will be served shortly."*

Tesh wondered, *Dinner? On a two hour flight?*

His neighbor snickered. "Two hours? Not in this weather, mister pilot man."

Jesus, will you shut the hell up!

Unfortunately, his plump neighbor continued to chatter as the plane set off from the gate and rolled down the tarmac. Tesh closed his eyes and clenched his ass. He hated flying, every damn thing about it, especially takeoff. He gripped the arm rests as the plane's nose lifted higher, all while his neighbor—"I'm a pilot myself, you know?"—narrated the plane's every function.

After several minutes, Tesh finally began to relax. He slowly opened his eyes. Though the plane was steadily ascending, it had not yet straightened itself, still curving slightly left as the pilot established their course. Relieved, he closed his eyes once again and breathed deeply. They were finally up in the air, and that's all that mattered.

"Yes...that's all that matters."

The whispery voice startled him. Had he spoken out loud? He didn't think he had. As the plane finally straightened, and he felt more secure, Tesh sat up and glanced about the cabin. Most of the passengers, like him, quietly clutched their seats as the plane continued up to its twenty-five thousand foot mark. He also noted several people sleeping soundly in their seats, unaffected by the travel. He envied them.

Someone grabbed his wrist.

Startled, Tesh quickly turned to find the young man in front leaning over his seat, locked on to his arm.

The young man groaned. "So...*hungry*."

His features left Tesh speechless. Through his damp blond hair, his skin was deathly pale, with eyes set deep in their sockets like shriveled grapes. His other hand clawed aimlessly at the plastic backing of his seat.

Tesh calmly tried to free his arm. "I'm sorry. I don't have anything for you."

The young man wheezed through his teeth, his eyes wide with disappointment. A thick line of saliva dribbled down his chin. He squeezed harder and pulled Tesh's arm closer.

"Hey!" Tesh yelled, pulling back.

From behind, the blond stewardess approached the young man and pulled him backwards, breaking his grip. His nails drug across Tesh's wrist, tearing skin. Tesh hissed at the pain. The young man moaned like an angry child as he threw himself back down into his seat.

"Sir," she said with a heavy southern accent. "You need to calm yourself and leave that nice man alone." She leaned forward and buckled him in.

He cried, "But I'm *hungry*!" and began punching on his own legs.

"Settle *down*, sir. You need to relax and close your eyes. We'll be eating in a little while."

Tesh thought, *Again with the meal talk?*

Once the young man was settled, the stewardess approached Tesh with a kind smile. "I'm very sorry about that. He's prone to occasional outbursts."

"You know him?" he asked, rubbing his wrist.

"Yes, Mr. Swartz is one of our frequent flyers. Are you ok?"

Tesh met her eyes. He then realized that, yes, she did look familiar. She looked so much like his mother: the same narrow-bridged nose and full pouting lips, close cut blond hair. Tesh forgot how to breathe. His eyes filled with tears. It suddenly became all too real.

When the plane lands, Mom won't be there.

Tesh slowly exhaled. "Yes…I guess I'm alright."

She began to walk away.

"By the way," he stopped her. "What's this I hear about eating?"

The stewardess turned back and stared blankly.

He felt stupid for asking. "Is there, like, an in-flight meal or something?"

"Oh." Her eyes locked on to his bleeding wrist. "Yes. Later."

Without another word she slipped away.

Tesh rubbed his wrist, confused by her meaning. Drinks, sure--but eat? *Maybe they mean pretzels?*

"I'd sure like to eat her," his chunky neighbor laughed, a bit too loud. "Woo-wee! Would you look at that sweet little Georgia peach?"

Tesh groaned. He wiped away the blood with a tissue from his pocket, thankful the young man had done little damage.

"So what do you do for a living, hoss?" his neighbor asked.

Tesh reluctantly answered, "I'm a, well, I'm a teacher. College professor. Literature." *More like* was *a college professor.* "But I do a little writing on the side."

The man scratched at his wreath of brown hair. "Write, huh? Like what—Penthouse letters or something?" He guffawed at his own humor.

Tesh rolled his eyes. "No, I write fiction. Mainly dark stuff like thriller and horror."

"Oh yeah? Well looky there—I'm sitting next to a big, fancy horror writer!"

The man turned to the window. The plane shuddered and lights blinked. "Well how about this for a story idea, mister horror writer man? The plane crashes, and everyone dies. End of story." He turned back. "How's that for a Times best seller?"

Tesh sighed. "Yeah…sounds like a winner."

"Of course it's a winner…but what the hell do I know about anything?" His neighbor sighed. "Sounds like you've got yourself a good job there. I'll bet you're real happy, too. I've got to tell you--and at this point I don't care who knows it--I'm not a happy kind of guy. And I'm not just talking about my wife—the cheating bitch—or my nagging-ass kids. It's my job that I hate, hoss. That's why I'm here, on my way to a production managers' conference, where I can't stand most of the stuck-up jerk-offs I've got to be there with." His eyes brimmed with tears. "I know I might not seem much older than you, but heed my wisdom. You've got to do what makes you happy. If writing and teaching makes you happy, well, then more power to you. I never thought I'd be in middle management. Hell, it's why I drink myself stupid before a flight like this. Speaking of which—"

He reached over Tesh and grabbed for the stewardess. "Hey, missy, could I get drink? Jack and Coke. I'm quite parched."

"Sure," she smiled. "And what about you, Mr. Hagman?"

"Nothing for me, thanks. Wait—how do you know my name?"

She was gone.

Something churned in his stomach. How the hell did she know his name? Like the ticket agent, he was positive she had no prior knowledge—and no damn reason—to know his name, last or otherwise. His skin began to itch. He suddenly wanted off the plane, away from everybody and their knowing smiles and negative observations. But there was nowhere to go.

"Nowhere to go."

Again that whispery voice. This time Tesh knew it wasn't his portly neighbor, or the stewardess as she came back to further his inebriation. His eyes narrowed as he glanced through the space between the front two seats. Eyes still closed, the older man in the window seat smiled as he repeated, "Nowhere to go."

Tesh leaned forward against his seatbelt. "Excuse me. Did you say something?"

The man remained silent.

Tesh tapped his shoulder. "Sir?"

The old man suddenly laughed, like a house creaking in a storm. "Nowhere to go…"

Outside, the sky growled like a startled bear. The plane jittered, then shook hard, jolting everyone in their seats. Drinks fell from tray tables, scattering ice about the floor. Startled, several passengers yelped as the plane took an abrupt hard right turn, then dove deep. From behind, a heavy *thump* was followed by someone's laptop as it slid across the floor. Tesh shut his eyes and tried to block out the scream of the engines. He grabbed for the arm rests, finding his right one occupied by his neighbor. Somewhere behind him a baby cried.

For a terrible moment, Tesh thought, *Oh God, please don't let me die!* Within a few minutes, the aircraft calmed, both inside and out, as the plane quickly straightened and pulled up. Tesh opened his eyes to assess the damage. His neighbor didn't seem too pleased.

"Damn it! I think I pissed myself!"

The rest of the cabin remained composed as they picked up their belongings off the floor. The others remained sleeping, unruffled by the sudden fall in elevation. All still wearing those damn smiles.

"*My apologies, ladies and gentlemen*," the captain informed over the speakers. "*On this flight, turbulence is to be expected.*"

Expected? Tesh unbuckled his seatbelt.

The older Asian stewardess approached Tesh from behind and gently pushed him back into his seat.

"Hey!" he cried.

"Sir," she informed, "please remain seated."

"Damn it, don't push me!"

Her tone hardened. "Sir, *please* remain seated. Dinner will be served shortly."

Tesh lost patience. He needed sleep, among many other things, and the fact she was pushing him back down sent him over the edge.

He sat up stiffly. "Now you listen here. Don't tell me what to do!"

"Whoa, whoa," his neighbor said, grabbing his arm. "You need to take a chill pill."

Tesh turned to him and grimaced. "The same goes for you, dickhead!"

The man threw up his hands. "You got it, mister writer man."

Unaffected by his threat, the stewardess buckled him in tight, like a helpless child. "Remain in your seat, sir.

Dinner will be served shortly." She patted his leg and turned away.

"Boy, what's up your ass?" his neighbor asked. "You've been awful antsy since the moment you sat down."

"Mind your own business."

"Now don't be like that. You know it's better to just let it out. I've already told you my sad story."

For a few minutes Tesh remained silent, letting his thoughts build behind his forehead. Finally, he sighed, "Not that it's any of your concern, but I lost my job about two weeks ago. I screwed it all up. I...I slept with one of my students and, believing no one would ever find out, we were caught by my TA. I was let go immediately. I've been living very quietly for the last few years since my wife left me, but since I have no second income--and the fact I haven't sold a story in nearly three years--I'm completely dry on money. Let's just say...I've thought about ending it all more than once.

"Two days ago, I got a phone call from the Orange County, Florida police. They told me my father is lying in the hospital in critical condition. They let me speak to him for a few moments, while he was half drugged up, to tell me what had happened. Sunday morning, as they were coming back from the grocery store, a drunk driver crashed head-on with my parents. Mom…well, Mom didn't make it. Dad is barely hanging on."

Please hurry, son. I need you.

"He managed to get a nurse to call me in a plane ticket to fly down and see him, but I don't…" He trailed off. "I don't think he's going to make it. He sounded so desperate on the phone, telling me to come down to save him or something. I just don't know what to do, you know? What *can* I do?"

The older man in front whispered, "I know what you can do."

"Well…shit," his neighbor muttered. "That sure is something."

From the corner of his eye, Tesh noticed the stewardesses walking through the narrow aisles, making sure people were fastened in their seats. He checked his watch. They must be getting close; somehow two hours had passed by quickly.

Somewhere up front, Tesh heard a cry and muffled thump.

Startled, he sat up to get a better look. The blond stewardess pushed him back down.

"Sir, *please* sit down."

Tesh growled, "I told you guys once before—"

"And we've told *you* once before, Mr. Hagman." Her finger jabbed into his chest, the nail biting deep. "Sit down and stay down."

Something had changed about her. Her facial features had hardened, narrowed in her aggressiveness, her professional touch gone. She didn't seem quite as helpful anymore.

His neighbor laughed, "I think she likes you."

Something wasn't right. He thought about getting up to inform the pilots of their co-workers' actions, but before he could protest, the plane took another dive, rattling the cabin. While those who still slept made no fuss, the rest of the cabin shrieked.

Within the racket, the old man in front whispered, "Just relax."

The plane curved left, throwing Tesh against his neighbor. The man grunted and tried to push him off. The wind howled against the plane, causing the aircraft to shift sideways. His neighbor's drink fell from his hand and hit the floor. Tesh grabbed his seatbelt and pressed the button. It was jammed. The woman across from him tugged at her seatbelt to no relief. She turned to him and yelled, "What the hell?"

The overhead speakers clicked. *"Ladies and gentlemen, I would like to take this opportunity to thank you for flying with us on flight 2110.*" The captain moaned happily. "*You've been a very pleasant flight, but now—*"

The cockpit door swung open. Dripping in blood, the captain stepped out holding the severed head of his trainee.

"It's dinner time!"

All around him, the cabin came to life. Those who had slept suddenly awoke. They shrieked loudly and leapt up from their seats, grappling with the nearest person. Passengers screamed and thrashed against their seatbelts as exposed flesh was met with teeth. Blood misted the air, spattering the white cabin walls. A screaming man bounded down the aisle, but was side-swiped by a sleeper and driven to the floor. Several overhead compartments popped open, spilling baggage to the floor. Near the front, a woman ran for the emergency exit and grappled with the handles before the captain grasped her and snapped her neck. The stewardesses greedily dove for her as she hit the floor. Tesh screamed and struggled against his seatbelt.

Outside, the storm raged on.

The young man in front of Tesh stood up. He threw his head back and howled. "*Finally!*" He dove over the back of his seat, covering Tesh's plump neighbor in seconds. With little struggle, the young man pushed against the man's forehead and exposed his thick, trembling neck. The man screamed as his attacker's teeth snapped into his neck and ripped sideways. A warm glut of blood splashed across Tesh's face.

"Just relax."

Tesh found the old man climbing over his seat, staring down at him.

"Just relax."

The old man pulled back his lips to reveal a pair of white gleaming fangs. His eyes never wavered, never blinked.

Tesh jabbed at the button on his seatbelt with no success, screaming and thrashing as the old man moved closer.

Suddenly, the old man was there, eye to eye.

"Just relax, Tesh."

The old man's piercing gaze bored deep into his own. Tesh suddenly felt heavy, sluggish. His panicked scrambling slowed until his entire body sank into the seat. His body not responding, Tesh swiveled his head to the side and closed his eyes. The man's oily mustache rubbed against his neck almost lovingly, smearing blood over his own face.

Somewhere behind him, the baby cries were cut short.

"I'm going to give you a gift, Tesh."

Tesh whimpered as the old man leaned in and bit his cheek.

The passengers continued to scream.

***

Dwight opened his eyes, finding only darkness. Something had woken him. But what?

Once again the pain hit him hard, like tiny mouths gnawing his nerves. He lifted his head and scowled, his only remaining arm shaking. Sweat dribbled down his face. Under the thin white sheet, he retrieved the trigger and jammed down the red button. Within seconds, the pain subsided. He caught his breath and reached for Margery.

He only found air.

Oh Margery, he thought helplessly, *why did you have to leave me?*

It had happened so quickly. An explosion of glass and metal. The stench of gasoline. Her head hitting the dashboard. He blinked once, and the image disappeared, leaving him alone in the dark hospital room, a mere shell of the man he once was.

What was he going to do? As much as he missed his wife, he didn't want to die—had no desire to join her so quickly. But he knew he didn't have much longer, recalling the nurses' grim looks and attempts at making him comfortable. They looked so dejected at his condition. His thoughts moved to his son. Dwight prayed he made it onto his flight. There wasn't much time. If this was the only way to settle his debt to that bastard Frank, then so be it. He just hoped Frank kept his end of the bargain.

The door to his room slowly crept open. Dwight grunted and turned his head.

Against the hallway's light, a man's silhouette stood in the doorway. Dwight narrowed his eyes, trying to find the man's face.

"Te...Tesh?" he croaked. "'Zat you?"

Dropping his bag, his son stepped into the dark room and slowly approached the bedside. Dwight looked up. Tears welled in the old man's eyes.

Despite the pain, Dwight lifted his only arm.

He exposed his wrist and waited for his gift of new life.

Story Notes

Ah, my first published short story. Granted, it wasn't supposed to be the first one (more on that later), but this was the first one released. I spent much of my first few years writing working on my novel *The Betrayed* and hadn't worked much on short stories. I was challenged by author Kelli Owen to write a vampire tale, and this was the result. It's not perfect. Had I written this story now, there are a lot of other things I would change and expand on that I didn't have the confidence to try then. As for the story itself, much of the banter between Tesh and his neighbor was real. I had taken a flight from Baltimore to Chicago, and my seat neighbor was just as overbearing and obnoxious as the gentleman in the story. He wasn't hard to remember when hashing out the details.

ARREARAGES

Cam literally woke up screaming.

The back of his skull buzzed angrily, causing his head to vibrate and his naked body to thrash about on the cold concrete floor he woke on. Every inch of skin called out, begging for the pain to end. He rolled over on his bare stomach and thrashed his legs, only now feeling the shackle and chain binding his right leg to the ground. The chain's clatter was barely audible over his howls.

He reached back and clawed the nape of his neck.

Something small and rectangular had been sewn beneath his skin. Something that trilled against the bottom of his skull.

Cam grabbed his ears and pulled them as hard as he could, yanked on fistfuls of hair, bit his tongue—anything to take his mind off the repetitive pulses. He managed to pull himself up to his elbows as vomit shot from his mouth. After his stomach emptied, his arms gave out, and he fell face-first into his own warm bile. His elbow struck something on the ground. He reached out and grabbed the item. A rusted steak knife.

He turned the six-inch blade over in his grip and, before he could talk himself out of it, he quickly ran the edge over his neck. The pain was glorious and nearly made him pass out, but he continued to rub the knife back and forth, deeper and deeper, until it reached the buzzing object. Blood sprayed and dripped down his neck. He dropped the knife, then carefully edged his fingers into the incision, gripped the edges of the object, and pulled. It made a soft pop as it came loose and hit the floor.

Cam laid there for a long while, his breathing chaotic, blood and tears running freely. When he finally managed to roll over, his eyes locked on to the object.

"What…the...fuck…"

A cell phone buzzed against the floor, his blood sprinkling the dusty concrete as it danced. Cam's eyes darted about, trying to place where he was and how he got there. Other than a faint white light above, everything outside his circle was black. The air was stale and musty, with a hint of wood dust. A pair of tighty whities was all he wore. The chain binding him to the floor would only allow him a foot worth of walking distance, but he couldn't even imagine walking anytime soon. The pain, although subsiding, was still constant, reminding him of the gaping wound he'd created with the only thing not anchored to the floor. He could not look at the knife…but the cell phone was a different story.

He picked up the phone and flipped it open. "Who the fuck is this!" he screamed.

"Does it hurt?"

He pulled the phone away from his ear and stared at it, shocked that someone actually spoke back. The voice was soft and feminine.

"I asked you who the fuck you are!"

"And I asked *you* 'does it hurt?'" the voice spat back.

Her voice was very familiar. Too familiar.

"Tanya?"

"That's right, shithead." He could hear her lips form a smile. "I'm surprised you can speak a full sentence right now, you know, with all that blood running down your throat from screaming."

"Screw you, bitch! What have you done to me? Where—?"

"Do you know how long it took *me* to finally speak after what you did to me? To form a complete sentence? Ten months, Camy! Ten long, excruciating months of recovery!"

Even now he rolled his eyes at her pet name for him. "I told you I hate it when you call me *Camy*." He recalled the incident, only a year and a half ago. The long stretch of interstate from Evansville to St. Louis where his then girlfriend, Tanya, continued to run her mouth for nearly a hundred miles on the back seat of his chopper. The bitch nagged on and on, grating on every one of his nerves until he just couldn't take it anymore. He sped his motorcycle up another twenty miles per hour, then grabbed her by the throat and heaved her off the bike. She hit the ground and tumbled and flipped like a chunk of Styrofoam in the wind. Just another loose-lipped bitch in the long history of Cam Felton.

She continued, ignoring him, "The pain I'm giving you right now, Camy, it's only a minor fraction of what I've experienced with you. Two years of my life, and that's how you thanked me? Crippling me? Taking away my ability to walk, my vision out of one eye? You deserve so much more than that, Camy. You deserve all the pain the body has to offer…and we're going to give it to you."

Cam was barely listening, tugging at the chain attached to his foot. But the "we're" caught his attention. "Wait—what do you mean 'we'? Who else are you working with, Tanya? You tell me right fucking now! You let me out right now or so help me, I'll—"

"You'll do what? Hurt me like you've hurt every other woman in your life? Destroy my life like you've done to countless other helpless women? No, Camy.

Your misogynistic reign as Cock of the Walk is over. You owe us."

"Goddamn it, you stupid bitch!" he screamed. "I don't owe you a damn thing! Now take this chain off of me, and maybe I won't crack your skull open again!"

"I have to go, Camy. My turn is over. It's time you spoke to someone else. Ta-ta."

"Don't you dare hang up on me!"

The line went dead.

Cam stood on shaky legs and chucked the phone as hard as he could, screaming obscenities as he did so. The phone clattered to pieces somewhere in the darkness. He didn't even think to keep it to call for help. Anger and pain ruled his actions, adrenaline suddenly coursing hard through his veins.

That bitch! How could she do this to me? Wait until I get out of this mess and then she'll really pay...

Just as he took a step forward, another terrible buzzing ripped through the bottom of his foot. Lightning-like pain shot all the way up his leg, into his torso. He immediately dropped to his knees and fell into a sitting position. His teeth ground together, and his brain swam in his skull. More screams ripped through his throat. He pulled his free foot off the floor and turned it over. Another fresh, jagged scar ran the length of his foot, puss-filled and raw.

"Jesus Christ! Not again!"

He quickly found the knife he'd used on his neck—a wound only temporarily forgotten—but this time hesitated. He didn't want to slice himself open again to bleed out, but what choice did he have? He pressed the dull blade, pushing down against the stitches. The area slowly opened up and more terrible pain poured red down his foot. He curled in his upper lip and bit hard to manage the ache, but it did little to help. The knife continued to slice through the tender muscle until it reached yet another vibrating phone. Only this one wouldn't budge. It was stuck to the bottom of this ankle bone. His hand twitched as he slowly ran the knife's tip under the phone. Once it hit a solid area, he closed his eyes, prayed, then pulled up on the handle. Pain exploded in his foot as the cell popped loose from the glue that was holding it firmly in place. Cam once again dropped the knife and rolled around on the floor, yelling anything that found its way past his lips. Blood flowed heavily onto the floor.

His hand shook as he answered, "I'm going to fucking kill you—"

"You're not going to do shit, Cameron."

"Sammy?" he asked through gritted teeth.

"Ding ding ding! Hard to forget the voice of the mother of your child, huh, stupid? What's it been now…three years since we last saw you? Three-long-years since you've seen your son, since the last child support payment. Three years since you stole my car and then ran over my foot when I tried to stop you."

The pain in his own foot was so intense, it stuttered his breathing. "Sammy—"

"No, asshole, you listen! It's finally my turn to speak! You treated us like shit for far too long. You beat me whenever you saw fit, then stole my car and ditched us. You're a disgrace to men. And to fathers."

Cam didn't necessarily disagree with her. He would be the first to admit he was a piece of shit to women, always had been. Just like his daddy, and his daddy before him. But he was forty-eight years old—were they really expecting him to change his tune now? A little blood and showmanship and he's supposed to change his ways? These cunts were pissing in the wind.

He listened to her sniffle and cry on the other end. She asked softly, "Do you want to talk to him?"

"To who? That little pussy son of mine? Thanks, but no thanks. I'd rather cut twenty more of these goddamn phones out of me then speak to that pansy. Both of you can fuck right off!"

Her tone immediately hardened. "You scumbag! We're going to make you sorry, Cameron. We're going to make you regret every bad thing you've ever done to us. Each and every one of us!"

"No, bitch, when I get out of this, you're the one who's going to be sorry!" He proceeded to smash the phone into the floor until it was in several pieces.

Before he finished, another buzzing started up, this time in his arm pit. Needless to say, more pain erupted through his body. He carefully touched under his arm and slid his fingers over yet another carefully stitched patch of flesh. How many more of these were hidden inside him? How many more would he have to cut out, just to bleed and face the wrath of every woman he had wronged? With all of the women in his past…he was in for a world of hurt.

It was only then he noticed the numerous fresh scars all over his body.

Once again he grabbed for the bloody knife, and, not so carefully this time around, plunged the blade into his skin. Something in his throat cracked as he screamed, his voice hitting another octave, and he immediately tasted blood. More vomit arched up and poured down his face. The blade's dull tip sliced through the tender muscle until it reached the phone, which he quickly yanked out and answered.

"Let me guess," he wheezed. "Asa?"

"I hope that hurt as much as it did when you did it to me." Hard to mistake that thick Korean accent. The incident she was referring to had happened several years prior, when his then girlfriend, Asa, had accused him of screwing her sister. When smacking her around didn't work, a quick switchblade in the soft area of her side seemed to shut her up quick. The relationship hadn't been a long one, but it had definitely been memorable. He hadn't heard from her after that day. Until now.

"What do you want, woman? An apology? Fine! I'm sorry for fucking stabbing you! Ok? I'm sorry. Now let me out of here!"

"Nice try, *baegchi*. Try saying it a little nicer this time, like you mean it. *Jigeum!*"

"I'm sorry, goddamn it! I'm sorry!"

"Not good enough."

Within ten minutes, four more phones had to be dug from his body, each one going back further into his love life. He cut ex-wife Cassandra out of the soft muscle of his ass cheek—roughly over the area he kept his wallet—because of the thousands of dollars he had stolen from her over the years, even after the divorce.

A woman named Barb, who told him he had shattered her knee cap during a liquor store robbery he'd committed back in his late twenties, forced him to dig another cell out that had been super glued to the edge where his femur and patella met. When she hadn't given up the cash right away, he'd shot her and bound her to a wheelchair for life.

Morgan was a tricky one. Deep in his abdominal muscles, near his stomach, he found the fat girl who he had tortured in college for her weight. His torment forced her into bulimia, and she'd nearly killed herself doing so. He had no trouble remembering her while slicing through the thick layers of muscle, nearly an inch deep. By the time he found her he could barely move, let alone prevent his own fatty stomach muscles from bulging out of his incision.

When he finally pulled out Marie, who was wedged in the tight space between two ribs, he was lying in a growing pool of his blood and piss, barely conscious. Somehow, he had managed to not pass out during the entire procedure, but the pain was so intense he could only shiver in stunned silence as the woman on the other end of the phone screamed at him.

"You probably don't even remember me do you, Cameron? Marie Clegg? Your high school sweetheart?"

"I'm sorry," he croaked.

"Remember all those girls you cheated on me with? Probably not. But I do. I remember every one of those sluts. Hell, back then you'd fuck anything with two legs and a big round ass."

"I'm sorry," he repeated, blood drying on his lips.

She laughed. "Oh, I'm sure you are. I'm sorry, too. Sorry this didn't happen sooner. If I hadn't been so weak and needy back then, I would have found some way to do this a long time ago. I dreamed for years after we broke up about causing you some kind of harm. I fantasized about hurting you as much as you hurt me. You broke my heart, Cam. Remember what you said back then? You said I was the only girl for you. You said you wanted to run away with me and get married and have five kids with me. Do you remember that? I sure as hell do. You destroyed me, Cam, and I've always wanted to do the same to you."

Tears rolled down Cam's cheeks. "Please…"

"It was a brilliant idea when she came to us about it. Really, I wish I would have thought of it."

"Please…stop…"

"Oh, don't worry, dear, there's only one more girl you need to speak to. The one who came up with this entire thing."

"What…who…?"

"Sarah Masters."

What was left of his brain function attempted to recall the name. Nothing rang a bell.

"The girl you *raped* your freshman year of high school."

Cam's eyes went wide.

"It's been over thirty years but she's been dying to speak to you…"

With what little strength he had left, he sat up and propped himself on his elbows to stare down at his crotch.

It began to ring.

<u>Story Notes</u>

To be perfectly honest, I can't remember where the idea for this one came from. It's probably my most violent story to date. I remember wanting to write it really badly, but I had nowhere to send it to. Most small press magazines and e-zines aren't looking for stories quite this extreme. In stepped Brian Keene. He got in touch with me back in 2014 to see if I would be interested in giving him a story for an e-book he was putting together to benefit a mutual friend of ours who was having health problems at the time. Of course I wanted to help, and it finally gave me a reason to write the story. I'd love to see this as a short film.

HE LOVES ME NOT

The first time I saw Dave Brewland I was awestruck. Such a big man and so utterly handsome. He stood much taller than myself, his thinning, russet-tinged hair smoothed back over his head—with just the perfect amount of gel—in order to cover his ever-growing bald spot. But that was no matter. I knew I *had* to have him.

I can recall when I first laid eyes on the stout gentleman, down at the pond near his home. He was fishing and chugging cans of God-knows-what with his two buddies, while I was gliding daftly through the cool summer water with the blue gill. I intended to catch one for my own benefit, but the moment Dave stepped out from between the trees and into my open sights…well, I was speechless, fish long forgotten. I was zoned in, spellbound by his walk, his talk, the gracefulness of every forehead-crushed beer can lying crumpled by his godly feet. Though a bit on the chunky side, he was perfect nonetheless.

I watched Dave from a distance, contemplating how our introduction might go about. Yet none of the titillating scenarios I conjured would ever work. If I were to swim up next to him, he would more than likely be frightened by my forwardness and toss me aside as if I were trash. I couldn't let that happen. I would be devastated, crushed in more ways than one. Though I wanted nothing more than to rage in my frustration, I had to remain calm, steel for the right moment to present itself. It had to be...*perfect*.

Then I saw my opportunity.

He caught his fish, and I tagged along home.

I stayed with Dave for quite some time—months it seemed!—but it took him even longer to acknowledge my presence. I felt as if I was being ignored, and I did not like it, not one bit. Why I was so surprised, I'll never know. They always ignored me at first.

It was rounding out to nearly a year when he finally began to notice me, the traces I left behind. And believe me, he wasn't happy—he was downright frightened for his life! I'm not sure why I scared him so badly. I tried to be gentle, I did! When he started to take more *precautions*, I simply laughed. Apparently, no matter what he did, it wouldn't alleviate the *pain* that I caused him, as he so *lightly* put it. Silly man. No matter what, I held on tight. I wasn't giving up that easy!

You must understand, I enjoyed being with him and holding onto him, embracing his all. I'm a tad clingy. But that was yet another problem: Dave didn't like clingy. In fact, he didn't like me at all. I fattened up while he shrank down, slimming to nearly a quarter of the size he was before we met. I thought it would have been for the better, but he didn't seem to think so. There were a lot of things we didn't see eye-to-eye on. His skin gradually took on a dull, yellowish wooden tone, and his teeth were wholly stained a blackish-green from continuous bouts of vomiting, the swarming stench of decay wafting from every hot, rank breath. He wasn't much of a looker from that point on--but I never left. I guess I'm a bit selfish, the whole "His loss is my gain" thing. Love will make you do crazy things. Anything to survive.

My love for Mr. Brewland dwindled down after several years and ultimately died when he last tried to rid himself of me. He made us both sick that time, and it angered me something fierce. After *all* that we had gone through, he still couldn't accept the fact that we were going to be together for a while—hell, for *life*, if I said so! Oh, well. It was sad, I must say, but I had to devour Dave much sooner than originally planned.

You know the old saying: The quickest way to a man's heart is through his stomach? Well, let me tell you right now it is absolutely true! Even though I started out in there, and had a bit of trouble inching up his raw, trembling esophagus, and chewing through its thick red walls, it was well worth it.

His heart was delectable.

And if anyone knows an easier route for next time, could you let me know?

<u>Story Notes</u>

Another early one. I really enjoy writing flash fiction. I find it a fun challenge to be able to tell a full story in five hundred words or less (granted this one is around seven hundred fifty, but you get what I mean). This one spawned after coming up with the final paragraph first, then it built out from there. My father said this is still his favorite of my stories.

BY THE THROAT

Roman shuddered as her nails found the small of his back.

This is it, he thought, cringing. *She's touching me again.*

In a terrible lapse of memory, he'd forgotten to wear his shirt to bed, the one with the high collar. It was the only thing that saved him from her touch…her needs. But with his bare back now exposed—and his own needs to eventually be satisfied—he wasn't sure if he'd have the strength to stop her.

Goddamn her, he didn't want it. Not tonight. If given the choice, not ever again. After their last time, he was finished with his wife's foreplay, her rambunctious love making, and her unruly hands.

In moments, her fingers slinked up his back like the delicate legs of a spider, forcing Roman to tremble—

Oh Christ, she's almost there!

—then abruptly gag.

"Goddamn it, Roman!" Gail yelled. Roman nearly cried tears of joy when her fingers left him. He curled up, shuddering at the thoughts of what could have been.

"You weak piece of shit!" Tossing aside the covers, Gail threw herself out of bed, as angry as he'd ever heard her. "This is absolutely ridiculous, do you hear me? *Ridiculous!*"

Roman wanted to scream, to lash out. She knew better. She knew his weakness from day one—but did that ever stop her?

Had it ever stopped anyone from touching his throat?

Doctors called it *Pnigophobia*, the fear of suffocation and choking. Roman called it his ruin. But his trepidation of rough fingers around his throat was not unwarranted. There was a time in his life where a much younger Roman spent his days playing records and kicking bullfrogs around the creek behind his house. The sun seemed much brighter back then, and the nights far more peaceful. The nights before Cammi, his adopted sister, used his neck as a stress reliever. For years his older sister tortured him, bringing him closer to death than the night before. Even now, years after she died from a brain aneurism, the memory of her voice still brought him to tears.

How long can you hold your breath?

Does that hurt? Does it?

Don't scream, little boy, don't you dare fucking scream.

That was only the beginning.

What his older sister had started, Roman found no end to. As a child, he was constantly terrified for his life, overly aware of the space between his chest and head. He had trouble sleeping, for fear of Cammi's hands, and to have his head lying back, neck exposed, was completely out of the question. Everyday actions like hugging and kissing became a struggle. Girls never stuck around. Friends left him. His parents, blissfully unaware of Cammi's cruelty, had thought their son was moody and unhappy, and his frequent outbursts did little to help their views.

Roman wanted to believe marriage would change him, but it only intensified his fear. The act of love making proved to be nearly impossible, continually straining his relationship with Gail. Luckily for him, Gail wouldn't quit easily. For years she attempted to help him, was supportive, even accepting of his phobia. Still, love couldn't conquer all. With the birth of his twins, Scott and Harrison, a whole new set of challenges emerged. Children with their tiny hands. Always *pick me up, hold me, hug me.* Why couldn't they just leave him be?

"Are you even listening to me?"

Gail smacked at the bed, snapping Roman back to reality.

"Listen to me, you stupid bastard!" With a quick jerk, she ripped the comforter from the bed, exposing Roman to a room constricting with her anger. He groaned, curling tighter into himself.

"I've had it, Roman," she growled, crawling up behind him. Her breath was hot against his back. "I've put up with your nonsense for thirteen years. *Thirteen years!* Every single day I've been patient with you. I've listened to your whining, gave you alone time, space when you needed it. I've even managed to distance your children from you, so—God forbid—they wouldn't touch or kiss you, or do anything that might resemble some sort of *normal* relationship. And for what? Just so you can stay inside your little fear-filled bubble? All by your lonesome? Well, I've had it!"

Gail climbed off the bed. "How does it feel? Knowing that you've driven your own children away from you? That your parents don't even speak to you anymore? You're a goddamn stranger in your own house—in your own life! And all because of that neck of yours... Pathetic."

Roman was disgusted with her words. But even more disgusted with himself. How long had it been since he'd spoken to his parents? Been invited to a party? Had he really been that selfish? *My little boys*, he thought. They were growing up so fast. Not long before

they were old enough to start forming their own opin-
ions.

What will they say about their old man?

Gail searched for her slippers. "This is the last straw.
I thought—hey, maybe I would try one last time and help
you forget your problem, and maybe we could beat this
thing, but obviously I was wrong. I guess we were all
wrong to help." She located her shoes and sat on the bed
corner to slip them on. She laughed harshly. "Well
don't you worry, my loving husband. We'll all be gone
shortly."

Shivering, Roman broke from his paralysis and rolled
over toward his wife. He was surprised to find her nude.
He stared, taking her in as though he'd not seen her in
years. She was still beautiful. Though her patience had
been stretched to its limit, Gail remained as attractive as
the day they'd met. Maybe a few pounds heavier, with
stretch marks she still complained about. Her blonde
hair had grayed some. And those wrinkles—had *he*
caused those?

She stood up and slipped on her pink robe. "I
should've listened to everyone. They told me to never
marry that—that *freak*! I'm sure I can find someone
else. A real man to satisfy me."

Roman cringed, her words burning his core. Was she
really going to leave him? The contemplation of her not

sharing their bed was terrifying, but the thought of her sharing someone else's, in someone else's arms...

Gail stomped toward the door.

"Wait!" Roman quickly sat up.

Gail stopped and slowly faced him. Her eyes spoke in volumes. "No. This is done. We're through! I may never get these last thirteen years of my life back, but I'll be damned if you're going to waste another minute of my time!" She moved for the door.

Roman lunged and snatched her wrist, pulling her back onto the bed.

"Let me go," she screamed, punching his chest. "Let me go, damn you!"

He snagged her other wrist, and held them both away from him. "Please don't leave me!"

"*Please don't leave me!*" she mocked, twisting in his grip. "You're ridiculous."

"I'm sorry, Gail. I'll do whatever you want—you name it! I'll get help, I swear. I'll do anything. Just don't leave me!"

Another of her harsh laughs flattened him. "Help? We've been trying to help you for years, and all you do is collapse deeper into yourself. Face it—you're help-less!"

Roman panicked. He had to think of some-thing—anything to keep her from leaving. Who else would have stayed this long?

"There has to be something I can do? Something to make you believe in me again?"

Gail sneered. "Roman, there's nothing in this world—"

Before he could turn back, Roman quickly lifted her hands and placed them around his neck. Gail gasped and immediately stopped struggling. Dropping his grip, Roman's eyes stayed tightly shut, wondering, *What have I just done?* His entire body quaked, stomach clenched, neck bobbing. Several seconds passed before he finally managed to breathe. Though his eyes were shut, he could only imagine Gail's stunned expression. *Keep breathing, keep breathing!* He counted every finger around his throat, from one to ten then back again, over and over—

But nothing happened.

For the first time in his adult life, Roman felt some-thing strange. Something like *happiness*. True elation at his revelation. She wasn't there to hurt him. May-be…maybe no one was. Roman sighed and slowly relaxed against her hands. Though his fears were far from over, this was surely the beginning of something wonderful. The first big step to the start of a new life.

Things could only get better from here. After this, no one could hurt him.

Roman opened his eyes. Tears fell down his cheeks.

Gail's wide stare was glued to her hands, her mouth in a small O. Almost lovingly, her thumbs stroked his Adam's apple. She was just as surprised as him, he knew it.

He managed a shaky grin.

Gail looked up. Then her eyes narrowed as she gave a small, wry smile—

And began to squeeze.

Story Notes

Where *He Loves Me Not* is my dad's favorite, I've always held this particular one near to my heart. *This* was supposed to be my first published story. It's got quite a back story, so try to stick with me for a minute.

Back in 2011, Cemetery Dance Publications ran a contest on their message board asking for stories of two thousand words or less. The stories would be voted on by the other authors and fans, and the top three with the most votes got to be featured in an upcoming chapbook, which featured the likes of Brian Keene, Ray Garton, and Douglas Clegg. Of the hundreds of submissions, I was voted into the top ten but didn't make the final cut. One of my close friends did make it, and I was really stoked for her. Almost immediately after the contest ended, I found an open call for stories from Indiana writers. I was accepted immediately, and kept regular communication with the editor (who shall remain nameless). When the book came out, I purchased numerous copies of the anthology and was going to have them with me at my reading slot at Horrorfind Weekend 2011 in Gettysburg, PA. I remember getting the big box in the mail and opening it up…and my heart broke. The editor, without my knowledge, rewrote my story from beginning to end. He took it upon himself to restructure every sentence, add a sexual subplot that didn't belong, and changed the technical term for my protagonist's fear from *Pnigopho-bia* to *Strangulophobia*. I was irate, to say the least. I remember emailing him immediately and asking him why he did this. He countered with how he knew better than me, how it was within his rights to do what he did, and how he could relay me to his other writing friends to prove I was wrong. I was so upset, but I countered him with the contract that we both signed, stating how he was absolutely wrong and in breach of a clause in his *own* contract that stated the editor can only make minor punctuation and spelling error changes. Anything else needed *my* permission, which I certainly didn't give. I had him remove the story, and I moved on. I spoke to a member of a local HWA chapter and they told me some pretty crazy things about him and how they had to change certain bylaws to permanently keep him out. The lesson here, kids, is to do your research on your editors/publishers before working with them, know your contract, and always get a galley to review before it goes to print.

The story floated around for a few more years. I sold it to two different publishers that both went under before the books came out. I started to think my story was a publisher killer. Then I was incredibly fortunate to find it a home in the Horror World anthology *Eulogies II: Tales from the Cellar*, alongside the likes of Gary Braunbeck, James A. Moore, and Tom Piccirilli—all of whom I am a huge fan of. The book came out not long after Mr. Piccirilli passed on from cancer, and all of the book's proceeds went on to his wife to help with their medical bills. I'm really proud we did what we could to help.

And now that you've read these notes, which might be as long as the story itself, onto the next one...

MINOR LEAGUER

(Author's Note: This story is a prequel to the story immediately following it.)

Morse's eyes flickered down the rink as the smaller man skated in tight, crisp circles. The way his blades cut through the finely polished ice. The sound of his black composite stick meticulously handling the puck. His short, rhythmic breaths as he twirled around the faceoff dots. To a normal person it could have been hypnotizing, like ASMR lulling him to sleep. But Morse wasn't a normal person.

Normal people don't get stripped nude and bound to a hockey goal against their will.

Arms splayed wide, Morse's wrists were zip tied to the crossbar, his hands tingling and numb, and his ankles were knotted with rope and pulled apart as far as they could go. All feeling in his bare feet was gone, and his dick and balls were mercifully hiding somewhere in his stomach. His knees shook. Hours had flown by, and he wasn't sure how much longer he could support his weight.

At the other end of the rink, in his navy blue Adidas track suit, Sully Tritt made a wide arc behind the net before skating straight up the gut of the ice. Morse snapped his eyes shut and turned his head as Tritt skidded to a dead stop in front of him. A plume of snow showered his quivering body.

"Whew!" Tritt laughed, out of breath. "It's been a while. Forgot how hard this is on the knees."

"Please…" Morse cried.

Tritt popped his neck. "Ugh. I should have stretched before I came out here. God knows I'm not getting any younger, right? Middle age is a fickle bitch."

Tears dripped down Morse's reddened cheeks. "Please let me go, Sully."

"Now why would I go and do something stupid like that?"

"I don't know anything, man!" Morse's voice echoed throughout the empty ice rink. Other than Tritt and his large associate, Willy, standing awkwardly a few feet away, he only now realized how alone he actually was. The front lobby was as empty as the feeling in his stomach.

Tritt cocked his head like a curious dog. "Know anything? What are you talking about, Morse? I thought we were here to have some fun, man? You need to relax. I've got so much stuff to share with you! Check it out.

Did you know I used to be a professional hockey player?"

Morse shook his head, but it wasn't his answer to the question.

"Obviously you wouldn't be able to tell that now, seeing this dad paunch I've been growing, but yeah. Played my whole life. Grew up quite the stud. Drafted in the fourth round, man. Pretty solid for some redneck peckerhead growing up in the Show Me state. I knew I wouldn't be a first rounder, but fuck it, man, I got my shot. That's more than most players can say. I'll bet you didn't know any of that, did you, Morse?"

Morse didn't answer. He kept his eyes shut, head turned.

"Morse," Tritt said, sighing. "Answer me when I talk to you, son."

"N-n-no," he stammered. "I didn't know that."

"Nah, I didn't think so. Didn't take you for a hockey guy. By the way, are you cold? Personally, I think it feels great in here." Laughing, Tritt tapped his stick blade against Morse's shriveled genitals. "Anyhow…I busted my ass to get to the pro level. You have to realize, just because you're drafted doesn't mean shit. You have to keep working hard, you know? That pro contract isn't a guarantee. After a few years grinding it out in college hockey, I got my contract, and I played my way to the Triple A league. I wasn't that bad, man. Not at all. I mean, I probably wasn't going to make it to the NHL, but it wasn't for a lack of trying. You see, they didn't overly value guys like me. I was a smaller, skilled forward. They wanted those big bruiser types, like Willy over there." He nodded over to his silent accomplice. "That big bastard would have made a hell of a defenseman. But Willy can't skate…or stick handle…or shoot… You know, what the fuck are you good for, Willy?"

Willy chuckled and shrugged.

Tritt turned back to Morse. "You know what my favorite part of the game was, Morse? Yeah, I loved the action and scoring goals and whatnot, but what I really loved was the pre-game warmups. Wait right here." He turned and skated out about fifteen feet away from the net. From the ice, he lifted a small tan tote bag and turned it over. Dozens upon dozens of black rubber pucks tumbled onto the ice.

Morse cringed and felt his testicles crawl further up his body.

"You see, when you're playing the game, you don't get to play with every one of your teammates. You're only on the ice with four other guys. I loved skating out with the boys, hearing the fans cheer, taking shots—"

In the space of a blink, Tritt ripped a puck at the net. Unable to move, Morse yelped as the puck zipped toward him. He waited for the pain—but the deafening ping near his right shoulder told him the damn thing never touched him. The puck bounced off the crossbar and kissed the glass behind him before landing somewhere near Willy.

"For those twenty minutes," Tritt said, "All twenty guys stood on the ice, and we were a brotherhood." He took another shot, this one flying under Morse's left arm. It hit the net behind him and clattered by his foot. "We'd run through our line rushes, practice saucer passes, stretch, and then line up and take individual shots on the goalie." Another puck snapped toward him, this one barely grazing his inner thigh. "Although goalies wear a lot more than you right now to stop shots, they never flinched. Their whole job is to not flinch. It they flinch or close their eyes for even a split second, the puck will be behind them. It could cost the whole team the game, Morse." Tritt eyed him, smiling beneath his mustache. "Do you think you can keep your eyes on the puck?"

Morse whimpered. "Please…"

"Let's play a little game, Morse. I'm going to shoot at you, one after the other, and as soon as you close your eyes or look away, I hit you. Understand the rules?"

"No, please! Don't do this!"

Tritt put a gloved hand up. "Eyes on the prize, Morse." Then they came, like bullets they shot toward him, and Morse did everything he could to keep his eyes pulled open. The pucks ripped off Tritt's stick and tickled the net behind him. Though Tritt grunted with every shot, the act seemed effortless, each puck carefully placed. Morse's body quaked, and he felt his bladder give out. Without thinking, he threw his head up and cried.

Beneath him, Morse's left knee abruptly exploded in pain. His body gave out, and he fell slack against the binds. Something in his groin stretched and popped. The thin plastic zip ties tore into his wrists. Trickles of blood warmed his skin.

"You looked away!" Tritt laughed. The smaller man skated up to him. "You would make a terrible goalie. You also make a shitty dealer, so I'm not in the least bit surprised."

Snot dripped down Morse's face as he howled in pain. He didn't know if Tritt had broken his kneecap, but he knew he wouldn't be walking again any time soon.

Tritt asked, "You know what's funny, Morse? That's the same kneecap I got busted, man, so I feel your pain. Christ, I still remember it like it was yesterday. Game six of the playoffs. Twenty-nine seconds left. Funny how you can remember the little details. We were up four to three. The other team had their goalie pulled, so they had the extra skater attacking. All we had to do was keep it out of our net and clear the damn puck out of the zone. Twenty-nine cock sucking seconds." He paused, staring into the past. "This big bastard defenseman from the other team…he winds up at the blue line and takes the biggest Goddamn slapper I've ever seen. Now, you may not know this, but we're all pretty well padded and are able to block most shots. So I see this fucker winding up, and I start to drop to block him. And that's where I fucked up, Morse. I dropped too low, and that bastard's shot clapped me right on the side of my knee, directly in the spot where there's no padding. Felt my knee cap shatter like broken china. Worse than what you're feeling right now."

Morse attempted to stand, but his left knee gave out again. Bone ground against bone.

Tritt squatted down to Morse's eye level. "I spoke about brotherhood, Morse. My brothers picked me up and helped me back to the locker room. There were stick taps not only from my teammates, but from the other team. And the fans out in the stands? It may have been a road game for us, but they clapped for me, too. They knew I laid it on the line for my brothers, and they recognized me for it. Hell, I knew my career was over, but that was beside the point. Do you know what my team did, Morse? They went out and won that fucking game. Because that's what brothers do." Tritt grabbed Morse by the chin and forced them to meet eyes. "Can you say you would do the same?"

Morse answered him with pained whimpers.

"We're a brotherhood, Morse. I may not have my hockey team anymore, but I've made my own little team here. You might work for me, but you see…you're like a brother to me. I've known you for a real long time. We've had a lot of fun, we've seen a lot of crazy shit, but you know what? We've always stuck together. You're honest, Morse. More honest than any other guy who sells for me, but right now I need you to be the most honest Abe you can possibly be and answer one simple question for me.

"Where's Doug Brett?"

Through the pain, Morse ground his teeth and tried to steady his breath. "I…don't know, Sully!"

Tritt sighed and shook his head. "Come on, Morse. I just got done saying how honest you always are with me. I'm not stupid. I know when you're lying. You're not a liar. Doug Brett on the other hand?" He chuckled a dry, humorless laugh.

Morse had no idea what to do. Despite the pain, he was rife with another sort of agony. Doug Brett was his closest friend. They'd grown up together in the foster system, and he even helped introduce Doug to his wife at his birthday party all those years ago. The last thing he wanted was for his friend to get into the same line of work, but the guy was desperate and needed cash quick. He had no idea Doug would fuck up this bad.

"I don't want to do this, Morse," Tritt continued. "I really like you. A lot. You may not be my best guy, but you still make me a lot of money. But that's not going to mean a whole hell of a lot to me if you're bedridden with broken legs."

Morse cried, "I swear, I don't know what he did or where he is! You know me, Sully! You know I wouldn't lie to you!" That was a lie. He knew exactly where Doug and Shauna were, and he helped to get them there.

Tritt shook his head, biting his lower lip. He stood. "I'm really disappointed, Morse. I thought you were better than this. I thought I could trust you, man."

Knee bones grinding, Morse attempted to stand, this time finding balance on his right foot. "You can trust me!"

"No," Tritt screamed, his voice reverberating in the empty rink, "I obviously can't! I know that you know that Brett stole thousands of dollars' worth of product from me, and I also know you're fucking hiding him from me! Now tell me where he is, Morse!"

Stomach and emotions flip-flopping, Morse had no idea what to do. He didn't want to give up Doug and Shauna, especially after just having a kid. But he also enjoyed walking on two legs. He didn't want to cry again, his eyes red hot and dry, but here came the crocodile tears. "Sully...I swear on my dead mother I have no idea what you're talking about. I haven't seen Doug in weeks. Fuck!" His bad knee gave out and he collapsed to the ice, his shoulders popping at the tension. He raised his voice, trying his damnedest to hide his lie. "I hadn't even spoken to him since before the new year. The guy's a fucking wacko, man! Always beating up clients and shit. I stopped going out of my way to talk to him forever ago! Whatever he did is on him, Sully! I had nothing to do with it. You've got to believe me, man!"

For several long moments Tritt stared at him, and Morse began to wonder if his act was sinking in. Tritt didn't move, his face a new canvas waiting for paint. Morse forced himself to keep his eyes locked on his. Even after all the years of working for Tritt, as close as they'd gotten and were able to virtually tell each other anything, he never got the courage to tell him he hated his fucking facial hair. The guy was a wannabe Johnny

Depp, with a mustache and chin beard that didn't connect. He was surprised he didn't try to dread his hair, too.

After what seemed like an eternity, Tritt pursed his lips and nodded. "Ok."

Morse arched an eyebrow. "What?"

"I said ok. If you say you don't know about anything I'm talking about, that Doug Brett is missing and you didn't have a hand in where he's hiding, then I believe you, Morse. I'm sorry for wasting your time here today." Tritt quietly turned and skated back to the pile of pucks on the ice.

Heart hammering, Morse tried to stand again and failed. "Wait, Sully, what are you doing?"

Tritt carefully pulled another puck toward him. "I've a got a few more things to teach you today about hockey before we're done here. Did you know there are five different areas that a shooter can target for when taking aim at a goalie?"

"No! Please, Sully! Don't do this!" He panicked and pulled at his zip tie bonds, to no avail.

"You see, the one hole is just above the left shoulder—"

Before Morse could blink, the puck was off Tritt's stick blade, and an instant later he heard a loud crack. An instant after that, pain exploded in his hand. His middle and index fingers had been snapped, and were now touching the back of his hand. Morse howled in pain and once more tried to pull his hand close to him.

"The two hole is just below the arm, down by the thigh—"

Another shot, and his broken knee was struck once more with six ounces of frozen vulcanized rubber. Morse screamed again, this time feeling his knee cap shatter like glass.

"The three and four holes, as I'm sure you can guess are on the opposite sides."

He was struck on the inside of his arm, between his hand and elbow, and the fourth shot struck him square in the ribs. Bones cracked in his chest, and Morse's screams turned into labored wheezes.

"Now the five hole," Tritt continued. "The five hole is a goal the goalie just doesn't want to give up. They've got those big ass pads on their legs and that stick they're supposed to keep in position at all times. For a goalie, to give up a five hole goal is quite embarrassing." Instead of taking another wrist shot, Tritt turned sideways, wound up over his shoulder and slapped the puck as hard as he could.

A moment later, Morse's genitals detached from his body. If he couldn't scream before, he definitely could then. Below him, blood squirted onto the cold ice, and small wisps of steam floated up into his face. No amount of words would kill the pain, no amount of pulling and yanking at his wrists would set him free. He kept his eyes clamped shut, not daring to look at the mutilation between his legs.

Tritt threw his hands up high. "And he scores!"

"Offsides," Willy joked.

"Offsides? Offsides, my ass. Check it again, ref!"

Willy lifted his open palm and studied it. "Upon further review…it's a good goal."

Tritt fist-pumped at the news. "I may be old, but I've still got it, baby!" He pulled another puck to his skates and wound up for another shot. "How about we go for the hat trick?"

"Breaux Bridge!" Morse screamed through his teeth.

Lowering his stick, Tritt asked, "What's that, Morse? I didn't quite catch that?"

The pain was so intense he could hardly stay awake. Vomit burst from his lips and splattered the blood-soaked ice before him. When he finished, he muttered, "He's…in…Breaux…Bridge."

"And where, pray tell, is Breaux Bridge, Morse?"

His vision darkened around the edges, his thoughts firing in every direction. How did it come to this? "Lou…Louisi…an…a…"

Tritt repeatedly tapped his stick on the ice, and Willy quietly clapped his hands. "There you fucking go!" Tritt yelled. "Like a good teammate, you sacrificed your body so the team could ultimately win. You're a team player, Morse. I knew you could do it."

Morse let his head drop and closed his eyes. His last thought was spent hoping Doug would forgive him. He suddenly wasn't cold anymore.

"You get the name of that place?" he heard Tritt say in a tunnel.

"Yeah, boss," Willy echoed back.

Then Morse heard, "Goodnight, sweet prince…" before a deafening slap, and something small and heavy blacked him out for good.

Story Notes

If you couldn't tell already, I'm a huge hockey fan, so this story was pretty easy to write. Again, this story is a prequel to *Between Those Walls*, which immediately follows. Sully Tritt is only mentioned a few times in *Walls*, and I wanted to expand his background a bit more here. I'd eventually like to do the same to Warden Jerome Dempson. Who's that, you ask? Keep reading and find out…

BETWEEN THOSE WALLS

"I'm going to do it."

"Do what?"

"I'm going to get out, Chuck. *Escape.*"

Charlie Hale immediately choked at Doug's word, the lump of food stopping midway down his throat. The plastic fork fell from his grip.

Escape.

"Would you keep your fuckin' pipes down?" Charlie coughed, smacking his barrel chest. "Christ, Doug! You can't be sayin' that kind of shit out loud in here. What if someone hears you?"

Doug Brett took heed as he scanned the crowded lunchroom. In a sea of orange jumpsuits, the inmates ate and conversed noisily, while the anxious guards paced back and forth, waiting for the inevitable fight to break out. The new guys—or *Babies*—kept to themselves. Luckily, the men at Doug's table didn't seem to notice their conversation. They laughed loudly and chomped down their food, trying to make believe it didn't taste too bad. Doug knew better.

"Sorry, Chuck," he sighed. "I...just can't take it anymore. I hate this place."

Charlie laughed haughtily. "You think any of these sorry assholes want to be here? You think *I* want to be here? And quit callin' me Chuck, you know I hate that." He picked up his fork and downed another mouthful of something that resembled meat. "Just face it—we ain't goin' nowhere."

A grin slid across Doug's face. "Is that so?"

"It's fact, brotha."

Doug thought, *Now or never.* "What if were to tell you I know a way out?"

Charlie stopped chewing. "A way out?"

"Oh, yeah."

"How?"

Feeling a bit haughty himself, Doug sat back and shrugged. "Hmmm, I don't know…"

Charlie growled, "How, damn it!"

Doug slid his food tray to the side and leaned in close. He could practically taste Charlie's anticipation…along with his mystery meat breath.

"You remember Fred Smith?"

"Yeah."

"You remember how he always volunteered for laundry pickup every night?"

"Yeah."

"And how he always took a long time to get back with the towels and blankets for our block?"

"Yeah, yeah," Charlie waved, "what's your point?"

"Well, the reason he took *soooo* long was because he was digging a tunnel in the laundry room—"

Charlie blurted, "*A fuckin' tunnel!*" then quickly shushed himself.

"Keep your voice down. No one else knows about this. I'm the only one Old Freddie trusted with this oh-so-important info."

"And what info would that be?"

Doug popped his knuckles. "Smith was damn near seventy-five years old the last time we saw his stinking behind. No one ever asked him why he was always late bringing up the supplies. They figured he had a bad hip—he shuffled around a lot, remember? But I know what he was really doing...Tunneling out through the back wall of the laundry room. Check this out." He tapped the tabletop. "The hole is supposed to fall into a corridor that's a few feet below the first floor. Fred had said it was fairly tall, reaching up to the roof, some twenty or thirty feet. Most of the corridor held offices and bunks for employees who couldn't make it home until the weekend, but they closed it down and sealed it up some twenty-odd years back. Fred saw all of this before they boarded it up.

"If I remember correctly," Doug continued, "the corridor start's somewhere near the hole, then snakes through the back hallways that house those bunks, and around behind our cells. Then, after a few hundred feet, it hits a dead end—a brick wall. And do you know what's at the top of that wall, my portly friend? A nice little pair of unsuspecting windows they just so happened to forget to cover up. They face out of the south side, by the truck unloading bay. No fences around that section, either. As squeaky clean as a virgin's puss."

Charlie sat very still, eyeing him. "Well...what did Fred use to cover the hole with?"

"He managed to scoot over a dryer that was sitting beside it. Covers it real good."

"What did he use to dig with?"

Doug hooted. "Forks!"

"Forks?"

"Forks."

"Wait." Charlie held up a hand. "Aren't the walls made of steel or somethin'?"

"Remember when they took us all upstate for a couple of years so they could renovate with new layers of concrete and steel? Well, what they didn't tell us—or the public—was they ran out of time and state-funded money about three-fourths of the way through the process, which means some of the various sections weren't completed..." He grinned. "Like the laundry room."

A smile grew over Charlie's face as well, though his looked daring. "What about the layer of concrete behind the drywall?"

"Back in the day, they used to give everyone metal utensils to eat with instead of these bullshit plastic forks." Doug jabbed his fork into the brown substance on his plate, which he guessed was meatloaf. "Fred would sneak two at a time when he'd go through the lunch line, so he'd have doubles. Then, when everyone would take up their trays, they'd give back their forks and everything would be hunky dorey, right? He kept all of his from over the years and stored them inside his mattress—spaced apart, of course—so when they gave cell inspections they didn't jingle-jangle all around. That's probably why he had back and hip problems, sleeping on forks all those years!" Doug chuckled.

"He'd take a couple with him every night and pick into the concrete, eventually wearing it down to the other side. It wore down pretty easily and, eventually, he broke through. That's how he got out."

Charlie slowly shook his head.

Doug asked, "What?"

"He didn't get out."

***

Every day his ten-by-ten foot metal and concrete quarters became smaller and less accommodating to his needs. A man required room to breathe, stretch—to scratch his balls without fear of hitting his elbow against the sink.

Space was only *one* of the luxuries he couldn't afford.

The moist Louisiana heat had dissipated during the later hours of the day, but the swampy humidity left Doug's mouth parched and chalky. He hated the South, had never gotten used to it.

When Doug wasn't in the yard or the Rec room, he was typically pacing his cell, recalling the last decade and the mistakes that came before it.

Though most of his youth was spent hopping from one foster home to the next, it was drugs and hard liquor that had become his surrogate parents. For years, he managed to cope with the loss of his real parents with their help, slowly burying himself into an early grave, but it was Shauna that had finally pulled him out.

Oh, Shauna...

He encountered Shauna Decker at a friend's birthday party, not long after turning twenty-two. The moment their eyes met he fell in love—ok, lust—but love came soon after. Everything about that dirty-blond country girl was perfection. Things quickly heated up, and within two weeks they were moving in together. The following six years were surprisingly smooth, even with his semi-regular drug use, which he managed to keep a secret. But with his criminal record, real job opportunities were nearly non-existent. The only work he could obtain was that which he was already deep into, so he kept on dealing blow to make ends meet.

No matter what he chose to snort or inject, his supplier, Sully Tritt, was far more hazardous to his health. Drug lord of eastern Missouri, Tritt was utterly ruthless in his practices, wouldn't bat an eye while pulling a trigger if he suspected you of stealing or skimming off the top…something Doug did inconspicuously whenever the chance arose. It wasn't as if he was *trying* to get himself killed, it was that more profit needed to be made, and with his end cuts after Sully's was in hand, there wasn't much left for himself. Shauna's job bagging groceries didn't offer much, so it was up to him to keep the roof over their heads—and with a baby soon on the way, the situation refused to ease up. It's a hard-knock-life when the rent was due and your gas gauge was on E. So when forty pounds of prime powder suddenly went missing, the fingers were pointing at Doug.

Doug promptly earned a new title: Dead Man.

After explaining to a very upset Shauna about his—*their*—new-found predicament, she led them south to the swamp lands of Louisiana, where her parents owned a plantation home they could hide in for the time being. It seemed like a good idea: hundreds of miles between him and his pursuers. The safety of his soon to be growing family was all that mattered.

Only they hadn't gone far enough.

That was over ten years ago.

Her screams fading like the heat, Doug touched the scar on his neck and grimaced. Once more, his eyes shifted from wall to wall, noting his all too familiar surroundings. A dilapidated bed hitched in one corner. A shit-stained toilet bowl in the other. No window.

The last piece of earth you'll ever live on, he thought miserably.

But there was one item that seized his attention: a white envelope. It was not as if he wasn't expecting it. Every month for the last ten years he'd waited on pins and needles for the single letter addressed for his eyes only. In the letters, the carefully worded text of Shauna's current condition, in her doctor's handwriting, as she lay comatose two counties over. As part of his desperate plea to the judge, Doug was reluctantly granted these updates, though they never truly put his mind at ease. The doctor's words were beginning to worry him. Though still on time, they seemed less detailed by the month, as if they'd given up hope, and with the last letter Doug's worst nightmares had come true.

They didn't expect her to live much longer.

The current correspondence remained as it came to him. Untouched. There on the floor. For fear of what it would say this time.

That's why he needed out—why Fred's hole was his only option. He had to see his woman, his Shauna, one last time before...

Depressed, he shuffled up to the bars of his second story cell and pressed his face against the cold steel. On the bottom floor, with several officers keeping rank at his side, Warden Jerome Dempson ambled into view as he led the *Babies* through their inaugural tour of the facility. Under a tweed dress coat, Dempson's rotund stomach protruded over his perfectly ironed khakis and shadowed a pair of polished white dress shoes. A thick mat of slick black hair combed flawlessly back over his head.

The man exuded arrogance.

"This, gentlemen," the warden declared in his thick southern drawl—an accent perfectly fitting for wine tastings and Klan meetings, "is where you'll be stayin', Cell Block numba six. Some of you fellas longa than othas, and some of you fo life." He turned to face the quivering group. "Now let me give it to you shawt and sweet, as I am a busy man and do not have the time nor the patience to *dilly-dally* with the likes of such...Iowa life forms as yourselves. Even your odor deeply offends me. You now reside in my house. You are my children and I am your daddy. You will obey my rules or else you will be punished—it's as simple as that. Do y'all understand?"

"Yes, warden," the group answered.

"Good." He gently patted his brow with a handkerchief and smacked his lips. "Now that we've got that covered, I would like to reiterate my stance on *es-cape-ees* and the like. Gentlemen, it will not happen. In my fifteen long, tireless years as warden of this here fine correctional facility, I have only had *one* successful break out. Now I'm not proud of it—ah, hell, I hate to even have to bring it up to you 'cause it pains me somethin' awful—but since then I have taken such…*measures* to ensure it will not eva happen again. Not unda my watch. And if you try 'n do so—even once—I will personally make sure that you will neva see the light of day shine on your degenerate heads eva again. Is this understood?"

The *Babies* agreed, though a bit more timid.

"Nobody escapes my prison." Dempson turned and gazed at Doug on the second floor, and winked.

"*Nobody.*"

***

"Bullshit he didn't!" Doug nearly screamed. He pointed to the barred window high on the far wall of the lunchroom. "The old bastard is out there scot-free."

Charlie slurped his drink. "Just 'cause no one ever found him don't mean that he escaped."

"What the hell are you talking about, fat man?"

Charlie kept his eyes on his tray, his lips pursed. "Look, uh, never mind."

"Never mind what?"

"I don't know," he mumbled. "I...hear things."

***

The steady squeal of the laundry cart wheels did little to drown out his thoughts.

Doug Brett decided to shorten his rounds. He sped up his usual process of getting the blankets and sheets to not draw any unnecessary attention...but the call of the hole was almost unbearable. With a tight stomach, and even tighter fists, he had stolen a few seconds to peek through those hazy windows into the second room over, where the washers and dryers sat eerily dead. And in the far corner, right behind that industrial dryer, was his only ticket out. Just not tonight.

Maybe not ever.

Dempson had nearly made Doug piss himself earlier with his knowing eyes and implicit words. He'd been thinking about it ever since. Did the man know? Did someone hear his proposed plans? His conversation with Charlie was still as fresh in his head as the sheets folded on his cart. What his pal had said made a hell of a lot of sense, even if he didn't care to admit it out loud. Maybe his plan *wasn't* feasible.

After several hours of sitting on it, he ultimately elected to side with Charlie: it just wasn't worth it. The attraction of getting caught and tossed into solitary confinement was lost on him. On the flip side, there was certainly no chance for parole, especially not for what he'd been *deemed*. Time was not kind, or good behavior rewarding.

Doug sighed and continued on to CB5.

He began to toss a fresh blanket through a pair of bars when the overhead lights snapped on and the alarm system exploded. He yelped and immediately froze, while the man in the cell threw himself backwards. Like a whale's cry, the alarms echoed off the walls, up and down.

Doug knew exactly what they meant.

He shoved the cart and dashed down the hall.

When he arrived at the opening of his block, Doug abruptly halted. On the upper decks, every available guard was bustling about, calling and screaming at one another with shaking fists and stomping feet. From their cells, the other inmates chattered and cat-called. Doug quickly backed away into the hallway. His mouth went dry.

Good Lord, he thought. *Who grew the balls to run out?*

In an adjacent floor cell, Tyke—a beefy black man with massive tattooed arms—had his face pressed between his cell bars.

Doug whispered, "Yo, T, what the hell's going on?"

Tyke eyed him and frowned. "Shit, Charlie done up and skee-daddled."

"Wha—? What happened?"

Tyke chuckled nervously. "Yeah, they was givin' him a random cell check, ya know? The mothafucka looked like he went ape shit on the guard and knocked him out. Ya know that big bastard guard, Winesaffle? Then Charlie up and split like yestaday's shit, dog. I seen the whole damn thing! I don't know what got into his white ass, but where he's headin', shit, there ain't no comin' back, ya hear?"

Doug was speechless. Why in God's name would Charlie try to run out? Wasn't *he* the one trying to talk Doug out of escaping? Where would he—

Abruptly, Doug turned and sprinted for the laundry room with only four words to drive him. *Fuck it, I'm out.*

Tyke's voice echoed amongst the alarms. "Yo, Doug! Don't do it, dog! The fat man's crazy! The walls ain't safe! You don't know what's back there…"

***

Doug stared at him blankly, then asked plainly, "You hear things?"

"Yup."

"Elaborate."

Charlie sighed, obviously wanting to drop the subject. "I just hear stuff, *ok*? You know how there've been a few escapes over the last couple a years?"

"Yeah."

"And you know that none of those guys were ever found, right?"

"Yeah," Doug laughed, "that's because they're probably living it up in Cancun right now, elbow-deep in Spanish poon."

Doug found Charlie glaring. "Sorry. Continue."

"They *claimed* they never found them 'cause they never actually got out. I've heard some fellas say that the warden is keepin' them somewhere here that no one knows about."

Doug waved him off. "I've heard those bullshit rumors, too—but come on! We know they got out and split. They're hiding out somewhere—"

"That's a crock a shit and you know it!" Charlie lowered his voice. "Do you really think the cops wouldn't have found them yet? Even a couple of them? Give me a break. Look, we all know plenty of ways to escape. I hear about those stupid holes everyone whispers about. Even the guards occasionally talk about it like it's some big jail house conspiracy. But no one tries 'cause it's too risky, and besides—"

***

Hurried footsteps pounded in his direction, just ahead. Doug managed to quickly slip sideways into an open door and shut it before they sprinted into sight. He braced himself, waiting for the attack on the other side.

Behind him, someone shrieked.

He turned to see a redheaded woman in a nurse's outfit juggling a phone receiver. Doug lunged and cracked her hard across the chin. She collapsed, unconscious. He'd never hit a woman before, but he figured today was a day for firsts. Heart pounding, he crawled back to the door and listened.

Three shotgun-toting guards appeared and immediately stopped before colliding with two others coming from the opposite direction. In heated voices, they quickly relayed information, while Winesaffle, rubbing his scarlet temple, screamed obscenities regarding Charlie and what they were going to do to his balls once they found him.

Winesaffle's radio squawked.

"Come again," he yelled into the receiver. The guards stood there fuming, sucking in breaths. Winesaffle grinned and laughed unexpectedly. "Ok…uh huh. Gotcha. Out." He nodded to the others. At once, they turned and fled down the hallway.

Jittering, Doug stayed low for a few more minutes until the coast appeared to be clear. He cracked open the door and quickly set off toward the laundry room.

With every corner he rounded, he expected someone to tackle him and drag him, kicking and screaming, to places unknown. After the last, surprisingly unguarded, corner the laundry room doors stood before him like a heavenly beacon. Doug wanted to smile—freedom now so close it hurt—but held his exuberance at bay. *Focus!* his mind screamed.

Doug broke through the swinging double doors, shimmied around a tight corner, then shouldered open the second set of doors to the machine room—

—immediately regretting it.

Warden Dempson and several guards stood before him, weapons aimed at his head. Doug went rigid, quickly throwing his hands up.

On his knees in the far corner, Dempson examined the gaping hole, which was not much bigger than Doug himself. The massive dryer that had covered the opening was pushed over on its side, leaving a full view of his escape route.

His only way out.

"Douglas!" the Warden exclaimed. The short man groaned as he pulled himself up. "Come on, men, guns down, guns *down*. No need fo such measures."

The guards slowly lowered their rifles, exchanging awkward glances.

"Douglas, how are you on this splendid evenin'?" Dempson approached Doug and threw an arm over his shoulder.

"Uh…"

"Y'know, it truly is a ma'velous night, Douglas. The crickets are out just a chirpin' away, the 'squitoes are makin' fools of themselves, the moon is bright and purdy. They don't have nights like this up north, no siree. Just a perfect evenin'…but I guess you wouldn't know that, now would you?"

No, I wouldn't, you fat fuck.

"You see, I was outside eatin' some of my momma's famous cookin', and catchin' up on some mail n' such, but then somethin' happened, Douglas, somethin' just *awful* that required me to be roused from my evenin' meal and solitude."

Dempson, reeking of jambalaya, lead Doug to the hole.

The guards remained expressionless.

"Douglas, are you aware this perforation in my wall?"

The million dollar question. He studied the hole as if he'd never seen it before, jaw slack, eyes narrowed. A damp, musty odor wafted out, making him wince. True, he had never gotten a good look at it before, only a couple of peeks when he could spare a few seconds. The only thing that bothered him was the complete absence of light.

He shook his head.

"Hmmm," Dempson nodded, freeing himself from Doug's shoulder. "That's what I thought. Tell me, where were you goin' to in such a dag-gum hurry?"

Lightheaded, Doug shrugged. "I, uh, I don't know."

"You don't know, or don't want to tell me?"

He shrugged again, feeling nauseous.

"Y'know what I think?" He paced around Doug, hands clasped behind his back. "I think that you were goin' afta your good buddy Charles, that's what I think. Overwhelmin' evidence shows that Mr. Hale ran right in here and went through that there hole in my wall. Just like dear Ol' Frederick Smith. Oh, by now he's probably found those windows y'all be whisperin' about and pushed his way out.

"I'll tell you what. You're more 'n welcome to join him if you'd so like to." He held his arm out invitingly to the hole. "*I* believe the best course of action would be that you could just do your time like a man, Douglas.

You *are* here fo life, y'know? You must pay fo your crime to the world, in order to right yourself with Gawd Almighty." He snickered. "It must kill you to know that you'll neva be able to make it all up to that lovely wife of yours. Such a terrible way to go like that, dyin' all by her lonesome. And such a tragedy what you did to your po', innocent son."

Something in Doug's stomach collapsed. His hand immediately moved up to his scar. "Wait—Shauna's not dead! And Norman? How did you know? I didn't—"

"Oh, Douglas," Dempson *tsk*ed. "I know everythin' about *all* the children in my facility. Let's just say…I do a lot of readin'." He pulled an open white envelope from his pocket and tossed it to the floor.

Dempson faced Doug, who was staring slack-jawed at his letter. "What's it gonna be, Douglas? In or out?"

Doug considered his options. "Uh…in?"

Dempson's shoulders slumped. "Such a shame. It would have been fun to watch it catch you. But then again…"

"*It?*"

Dempson grinned, then turned and tapped Winesaffle on his shoulder. The guard, with a smirk of his own, stepped forward and dropped the butt of his rifle into Doug's nose. An explosion of stars filled his vision. Blood squirted across his face. Doug collapsed, wheezing for breath. Multiple hands clasped onto his clothing and began dragging him, unwilling, toward the wall.

The ground suddenly disappeared.

***

"Besides what?" Doug asked.

Charlie sighed long and hard, choosing his next words carefully. His eyes spoke words of their own.

"I hear somethin', between those walls."

***

Despite his best efforts, he could not prevent every bit of liquid from gushing up his nose the moment he plunged under. Blood mixed with warm fluid, burning furiously. He found the floor and pushed upward to break the surface. He gasped, eyes fluttering, thankful the water depth was only up to his chest.

"Looks like you had a nasty spill there, Douglas!" called Dempson, from above. "Mighty dark down there…smells a bit, too. Here. I think this might help you in your travels to redemption." He tossed a small object out into the water.

Doug quickly grabbed for it. A small flashlight.

"And rememba, Douglas…the road to salvation is a wet one, indeed!"

He stepped back and the hole was immediately covered, blocking out the last bit of light. Once again, light ceased to exist within the world of the hole.

"Fuck you!" Doug finally screamed. His voice reverberated back, making the darkness that much more suffocating.

Doug clicked on the flashlight. Thankfully, the darkness had boundaries. Weathered concrete walls lined both sides, plastered in mildew and hairy patches of green fungus. The water—at least he *hoped* it was water—was late-night tepid and reeked of…well, *something* he couldn't quite put his finger on. Garbage? Waste? Pieces of black muck floated on the surface.

But why the hell is there water?

With not an inkling of where to start, he sloshed around the first corner and discovered a dim light set up high on the wall to his left. The bulb buzzed and flickered, but the glow was not strong enough to guide him. He turned and turned, searching for any signs of life, but was only faced by more inner-leading concrete. The further he pressed on, the water grew deeper. After a while, he was forced to swim.

"Charlie!" he called desperately, hating the frantic whininess in his voice. The foul water lapped at his chin, and some managed to slip past his lips, making him gag. Despite the flashlight, the darkness crept in mercilessly, threatening to break his will.

"*Charlie!*"

A shrill cry rang out from behind.

Followed by a wall-rumbling growl.

Doug's flesh went cold. *"What was that?"*

Flashlight gripped in teeth, Doug paddled blindly around a few more corners and soon came across a small wooden platform bolted into the wall, a few feet above the water. He pulled himself up, wiping off the black slop covering his body, and found another hanging light jutting out above his head. He reached up and twisted the slimy bulb. The area gradually illuminated.

Doug gasped.

In the murky light, numerous bodies hung from the walls, chained up by hooks and massive iron links. Most of the corpses were so badly decomposed their faces had become indecipherable from one to the other. Though some were still whole, other hooks held only what appeared to be left over. Doug gagged, finally realizing what the smell actually was: the hot stench of rotten flesh. He threw himself back against the wall, covering his nose.

Something grazed his neck.

Doug flinched and quickly turned.

Heavy chains and hooks buried deep into his decaying flesh, Fred Smith was suspended just over Doug's head, his shoe level with his face. His bloated, bearded head was slumped over on his shoulder, eyes yellow and vacant. Through his horror, Doug noticed Fred's right arm and leg were missing.

They looked bitten off.

So much for the Spanish poon...

Another growl thundered from around the bend. Panicked, he unscrewed the light bulb and shrank down, hiding in the safety of darkness. After a few moments, waves sloshed as something large waded under the water ahead. When it reached the adjacent wall, a massive shape leapt up, dousing dirty water over Doug. The smell was overwhelming.

Even in the water's depths, the *thing* stood easily over fifteen feet high, with greenish black scales covering its enormous body. A rounded spine protruded over its back, a spiny tail bobbing behind it. In its man-like paws was Charlie, writhing as its nails dug through his orange jumpsuit.

The creature pinned Charlie against the wall, then stuck its bulky arm down into the water and pulled out a handful of chains. Charlie screamed as the creature wrapped his weakened body. Finished, it snapped the hooks into eye bolts already set into the wall. Charlie wept and kicked his legs. The creature rewarded his efforts by pushing him until he swung like a pendulum. It *cackled* at its work, content.

Charlie slowly peeled open his eyes and squinted.

"D-Doug?"

The creature tensed, then whipped around his elon-
gated head and growled. Without thinking, Doug stood
and clicked on the flashlight, and with a trembling hand,
pointed up.

There it was, that same old feeling bubbling deep in
his gut—a roil of stomach and tightness of ass. The
same unforgettable feeling that had ruptured over his
being when Sully had found them and indefinitely
destroyed his life.

With thinly slitted pupils, the corner of the creature's
snout shifted into an impossibly wide grin. Long, rotten
teeth hung slack from its mouth. Deep in its throat, it
croaked with a low groan like someone bending wood,
and before Doug could move, it dove into the water and
disappeared.

Heart thundering, Doug looked back up at Charlie.
He swayed slowly back and forth against the flashlight's
beam.

"Charlie," he moaned.

Black water erupted as the creature shot up and
swung its fist, shattering the wooden platform. Doug
flew sideways and landed on his back in the water,
driving the air from his body. He resurfaced and gasped,
flinging water from his face. The creature quickly
located him and began gliding in his direction. Without

thinking twice, Doug swam with everything he had—moving for what seemed like an eternity, rounding many darkened corridors, but never seemed to find anything but a deeper blackness his flashlight refused to penetrate. His heart bobbed in his throat, breaths coming in short bursts. Doug grabbed at the walls, but his fingers slipped through the clinging slime.

As he swam along the wall, his foot brushed against something hard. He quickly dove under. Through the debris, he found a doorknob, then the outline of a door. He resurfaced, finding the beast coming up fast. Doug dove back down, gripped the knob, and pushed as hard as he could. When it wouldn't budge, he started kicking. The creature rapidly closed in. Finally, the door flung open and immediately sucked him through.

Head over heel, Doug tumbled in and crashed into a small desk. Water surged into the tiny bunk room, sloshing over the two small beds in the corner. He stood, frantically searching for a way out—

—the water rising to his chest—

He turned in every direction.

—then splashing at his neck.

I can't die like this!

As it went over his head, he located a small window, no bigger than a pillow, on the far wall.

Something flushed into the bunk room.

A large spine rose to the surface, along with two beaming eyes.

Doug took a deep breath and swam for the window. With the flashlight's handle, he immediately thrust his hand through the water-softened glass—

—and the glass shattered, water surging in from the other side, pushing him backwards. He grabbed for both sides of the frame and managed to pull himself out against the rush, the leftover glass shards slicing across his midsection. The moment his legs pulled past the window sill, a massive scaled arm reached out and swept through the open water. Finding nothing but floating threads of blood, the creature roared and pulled its arm back into the bunk room.

Despite the pain, Doug resurfaced, sucking in a deep breath, and paddled away. He had to keep moving.

The water seemed different on this side, cleaner and less disturbed. There were still bodies strung up on the walls, but these looked untouched for some time—too rotten for even *it* to want. *This is it*, Doug suddenly realized. *This is Dempson's secret place! No solitary confinement here—you just become fucking alligator chow. No questions asked.* Who gives a shit about a bunch of lifers out in the middle of the bayou? They were there to die anyway, right? By someone's blade or something's teeth, when it came down to it, did it really matter how?

Not this guy. He had something to live for.

Shauna.

Such a terrible way to go like that, dyin' all by her lonesome...

No—it wasn't true! She was still alive, waiting for him at White County General.

The sudden image of Shauna's broken skull made Doug want to vomit.

"*Goddamn you, Sully!*" he screamed, slapping the water.

A faint glow illuminated his way from up ahead. The next corner presented him with a dead end. He nearly choked.

The windows.

"Ha! I win!" Doug yelled, elated. "You hear that, you big bastard?"

The brick wall behind him exploded. Doug spun to see the creature's massive body leap out and hit the far wall. It hissed furiously and dropped backwards into the water. Doug turned and splashed forward, pushing himself to every limit.

He found another platform directly under the window and quickly hoisted himself up. His arms shook and his nose burned. He looked up at the windows. At least five more feet up. He gripped the loose bricks and slowly urged himself up. Every grip sent lightning-like pain through his stomach. Blood pattered the platform below. He stopped for a moment to catch his breath.

Almost there, Shauna, he thought. *Almost there.*

A voice in the back of his head spoke up. *She's dead, you fool. Dempson already told you. Yeah, Sully found you, all right. You woke up in bed just in time to see him crank the final spin on the vise that encased Shauna's head. Remember how her body shuddered, how blood spilled from her eyes and nose as you screamed her name? Then he shot you in the neck, didn't he? Put you out for a while. Then he took a knife and—*

"*Shut up!*" he screamed.

At the top, he grunted and reached up, touching the cold glass with his finger tips. The moon stared back at him, questioningly.

Something splashed behind him.

Before he could move, the creature hit the wall and seized Doug's legs, springing backwards. Doug tried to scream, but only received a mouthful of water.

He tried to swim, but the creature came up from under and grasped him around his midsection. He was lifted from the water and slammed hard against the brick wall. His skull bounced. Blood immediately filled his mouth, drained from his nose.

The creature's head was even more massive up close, with eyes far too intelligent to be of this world. Once again it cackled, bellowing in the tainted darkness.

His mental voice spoke…*And after he left Shauna brain-dead, then what? What did he do with that kitchen blade, Doug? WHAT DID HE DO? He used it on baby Norman, that's what he did! And unlike Shauna, he didn't fail to take out your only son, did he? He wanted you to pay for stealing from him, make you pay dearly. And the grand finale? His prints weren't on the weapons. He took care of that. But who's were, Doug? Whose prints were all fucking over them when the cops found your family?*

Yours—that's who!

Shauna's finally dead, baby Norman's gone, and—

"Oh, God!" Doug moaned, throwing his head back. "I caused this! I deserve this! *I deserve this!*"

The creature grinned, knowing, and opened its jaws.

Shauna, please forgive me…

<u>Story Notes</u>

Let me tell you about the best rejection letter I ever received. Years ago there was a horror magazine called Necrotic Tissue, run by a great editor named R. Scott

McCoy. Early in my career I wrote him this story, which at the time was a whopping twelve thousand words. I got back a rejection letter some time later. Most rejection letters are form rejections and basically say *thanks but no thanks*. Scott's letter to me was several paragraphs long, and he took his time explaining what he liked and didn't like about the story. He suggested a lot of major changes, which all worked out for the best. I was really thankful he took the time to help me. I eventually sliced the story in half, cut apart the beginning chatter between Doug and Charlie and peppered it between scenes throughout the rest of the story, and sold it to another magazine. Sometimes rejections are a good thing, especially early in your career.

GOD BLESS YOU

Coolie didn't stand a chance.

Sasha burst through the doorway and dashed into the stairwell, screaming at Coolie to "*Fucking hurry!*" But he wasn't quick enough. The second his foot hit the threshold, the man in the black knit mask surged in from behind and jabbed his knife *one*, *two*, *three* times through the back of Coolie's neck. Coolie gurgled, blood discharging through his lips, and collapsed face-first to the floor.

Sasha screamed and nearly fainted, but managed to keep her momentum up the two flights of stairs until she reached the top. She collided with the single steel door and tugged frantically up and down on the handle.

Locked.

"*Nooooo!*" she cried, her banging to no avail. "Help me! *Somebody help meeeee!*"

The door below her slammed shut—the sound shattering her frenzied cries. The killer's footsteps—slow and calculating—teased their way up the stairs, one step at a time. Sasha bawled and beat on the door, her desperation reverberating against the concrete walls. Her legs went weak. She slowly sank to her knees, knowing this would not end well—

—but the moment the killer rounded the landing and up the next few steps, Sasha shot to her feet with a renewed strength and screamed for some-one—anyone!—to hear her. Fifteen feet away, the killer grinned through the hole in his mask. Blood smeared the perfect silver of his blade.

"Someone!"

Ten feet away.

"Help!"

Five feet.

"Me!"

Screams hitting their peak, Sasha knew escape was futile. She turned to face her death, cowering against the cool metal door that should have been her escape—safety only two and a quarter inches away—but it only felt like a vertical cutting board, waiting for his blade to scrape the other side beyond her flesh. "Please!" she begged. "Don't hurt me!"

The glint of his blade was his only response as he lifted it chest level and stepped forward.

A pressure built up in her throat, fighting to break surface, and just as Sasha opened her mouth to scream—

She sneezed.

Eyes closed, the killer grunted and stepped back, swatting away her snot mist with a gloved hand. Droplets peppered his black outfit, while several long green strands dribbled down his shirt. Sasha quickly covered her nose to suppress another sneeze, her eyes as big as saucers.

They both stared at each other in silence.

With his free hand, the masked man slowly reached behind him and produced a clean white tissue from his back pocket, offering it to Sasha. For a few moments she hesitated, then carefully took the tissue and blew her nose.

"Thanks," she mumbled, "that was very sweet of you."

The man nodded at her appreciation. He pulled a small baggie from his front pocket and had her dispose of the used tissue, then folded and replaced it back in his pants.

Sasha sighed, "Well…now what?"

The killer shrugged, then stepped forward and stabbed.

Story Notes

I remember walking up a flight of steps at my old job, the very steps of this story, and the idea hit me. I had to sit down for a few moments to laugh. I loved writing something completely serious, then go into something so absurd but playing it absolutely straight. It's fun to get a little weird in flash fiction.

HOME INVASION
(WITH NIKKI MCKENZIE)

"...and that was the third time I caught the Clap!" Cooter squealed and slapped his dusty knee.

For the fourth time that day, Fisher managed to swallow the tidal wave of vomit before it burst from his lips. His stomach *rolled* at the thought.

"Boy, I'll tell you what, you better pray you don't ever catch that *goner-ree-a*. Nasty stuff." Every *S*, hard or soft, managed to wheeze past the gap between his two front teeth. "I had pus runnin' from the tip of my pecker like a leaky faucet fo' well over a month, and ma' balls went and swelled up bigger than a head of lettuce, too! After the doctor—who was a nice feller by the way—fixed me up with that...whatchamacallit? Tetra-something? Anyway, once he done cured me of that stuff, I went back ta' that old whore Frieda and said, 'You old cooze! You done gave me the dick snots!' And she came back with, 'Well, whadja expect, Cooter? Didn't you learn the first two times?' Can you believe the balls on the old washboard? Mercy, mercy, mercy..."

Eight hours. That's how long Fisher had been endur-
ing the non-stop ramblings of Cooter's "sexual prowess"
in the old man's eighteen-wheeler, on their route back
from Ft. Wayne, and for eight hours—the last few
rocketing down I-24 West through Nashville—Fisher
wondered how much of it was complete bullshit. He had
to have been damn near seventy, and it still tickled the
old fart pink to brag about every conquest from Albu-
querque to Syracuse. For the first few hours, Fisher
smiled and nodded, but several hours in—and several
upchuck close-calls later—he began to wonder how the
old, toothless bastard wasn't a walking herpes sore.
Fisher's grip tightened on the steering wheel. He was
dog-tired. Enough was enough.

"Hot damn! I haven't told you about the time I covered myself in peanut butter—"

"Cooter," Fisher stopped him. "Seriously, I've had
enough."

The old man glared at Fisher with a cocked, bushy
brow. "Enough, eh? Really, boy, you really wanna go
there? You know, the last I checked you were on proba-
tion with the company—skippin' out on work, wreckin'
a truck, never making it on time to your scheduled stops.
As far as Mr. Coscom is concerned—as far as Titan
Foods is concerned—they've had enough of your malar-
key. But bein' the sweetheart that I am, I stopped them

from shit-canning your sorry behind, and instead I get ta' watch you for a few months on your trips until you get your head straight again. Hell, I did it 'cause I like you. You remind me of me at your age."

Wonderful, Fisher thought.

"And don't worry about what happened back there at the drop. I won't tell ol' Coscom about you forgettin' to turn the cooler back on after stopping in Indy, spoiling all that food and the like. I'll take the hit on that, don't you worry. Ain't no way that bag of hot air is gonna get rid of me. But you just remember you owe me big time."

Fisher threw his head back against the headrest and sighed. All he wanted was to get home, pet his stupid cat, hold his fiancée Missy and the future little Fisher blooming inside her, and assure them everything was going to be ok. *It* is *going to be ok*, he repeated. He knew he'd fucked up time and time again with Missy—the lying, ditching work, and making side trips to Lexington for the horse track, blowing through the money her grandparents had gifted them for their wedding and their child in a matter of minutes—but he swore he was finished with all that. And he was. But Mr. Coscom felt the need to regularly remind him what a screw-up he really was, and his so called "gambling addiction" was a threat to the company's perfect record of timeliness. With Coscom's remarks and Cooter's rants, Fisher was damn near ready to drive the old man's rig right off the Tennessee mountainside. Lucky for him—and Cooter—he was careful at keeping cool.

The sign for the first downgrade before Monteagle passed by in a flash.

Not much longer, Missy. He glanced down at his cell phone in the cup holder. He wanted to call her. Bad.

But as much as he wanted to rush home, Fisher reluctantly pulled off the accelerator and rode the brake pedal as the interstate began to slope. His knuckles popped as he gripped the wheel tight, ass clenching against the seat. The big rig groaned as it pulled the empty cooler trailer behind it. He steered the truck into the far right lane, then clicked on his emergency lights, to let the rest of the smaller vehicles behind him pass. Their taillights bloomed in the darkness, lighting the granite mountain walls in bright cherry reds. Fisher kept his focus straight ahead and knew it was only a matter of time before the truck's buzzer would go off and they'd have to stop for the night. *Goddamn federal time regulations!*

"Hot damn," the old redneck giggled. "I can't wait to get back home! Been living in Chattanooga for almost all my life, probably same as you. Love that city. So full of history and beauty...and long-legged women. I always love crossing that ol' Nickajack Lake, 'cause you know it ain't but a few more miles 'till we hit that

Chattahoochie. You know, the way it sits in the bottom of that mountain bowl, so beautiful. It's like Atlantis...with Waffle Houses."

Something bright flashed overhead, momentarily blinding Fisher. Before he could cover his eyes, the light narrowed, then zipped past the front of his rig and smashed into the adjacent rock wall. Fisher screamed as he slammed his brake pedal to the floor. The brakes squealed in protest, and the trailer's rear end swung toward the left lane. Soda bottles and half-empty Frito bags spilled across the floorboards. An SUV blared its horn from behind. Fisher panicked and jerked the wheel to the left, nearly colliding with the smaller vehicle. Cooter yelped as his head slammed against the window. The SUV screeched and spun until it faced the opposite direction. Fisher righted himself but knew he was getting too close to the edge. He aimed for the emergency truck ramp and pumped on the brakes. Gravel and sand exploded across the road as the big rig soared up the rocky path. Fisher ground his teeth, fought to keep the rig straight on the path, and kept the brake jammed to the floor until the truck finally halted at the top of the incline.

"God damn, boy!" Cooter hollered, rubbing his head. "Did you see that?"

Fisher, arms locked against the wheel, finally exhaled. "Yes, Cooter, obviously I saw that!"

"Holy mother and Mary, that was brighter than shit! By the way, you better hope you didn't damage my rig, otherwise someone's gonna owe me twice!"

Cooter dug under the passenger seat until he found his Maglite, then leapt out of the truck and carefully crept along the rock wall. "Come on, boy! Get out here and let's see what you almost killed us over."

Knees shaking, Fisher reluctantly snatched his own flashlight and lowered himself out of the truck while leaving his cell phone behind. He jogged to catch up with Cooter.

Something glowed on the ground up ahead.

From behind, the truck's buzzer sounded off.

***

Several miles away on the outskirts of Chattanooga, Missy struggled with her own upchuck reflex. "Ew, Sondra. Don't say that."

Sondra peeked over the colossal coffee mug she held with both hands, steam rising over her face. "Say what?"

"You know what," Missy shuddered. "Ugh."

Sondra placed her mug on the little diner-style table in the corner of the soon-to-be Fisher family kitchen and smirked at her friend. "What? All I said was, 'Don't get your panties in a twist!'"

Missy shifted before the oven, back to her friend—a nervous, disjointed, twitchy sort of dance. The metal tongs in her hand waved through the air as if to swat some unseen fly. "*That*, Sondra! Don't say...*panties*."

She said the word with child-like embarrassment, spoke so softly the sizzling of the pork in the pan was almost louder. Her cheeks flushed, which had nothing to do with the heat of the stove-top, and she could not keep the grin off her face.

"Don't say that. Say *underwear* or something."

"Are you kidding, Missy? Panties? You can't handle the word *panties*?" Sondra said the word loud and hard, and Missy jerked every time. "How did Justin ever get *into* those panties?"

"Hey!" Missy turned from the oven, wielding the tongs at her bestie like a Catholic school teacher would a ruler at an errant child. "He got into them by being a *gentleman*, by being sweet and gracious and well-mannered. He could teach you a thing or two."

Missy caressed her growing belly, something she did instinctively at the thought of her future husband. Even if Justin was away, as was often the case, she could still feel him, in her, in their little one. She glanced down and smiled.

"You miss him."

Missy looked up to find her friend's big, green eyes probing, a soft smile on her face. "Of course I do. I love him."

"Oh, I know," Sondra said, nodding. "I can see it all over your face. And in that belly, there."

Both women giggled.

"When will you find out the sex?"

Missy put up a finger as if to say *wait*, moved the bacon in the skillet about—grease popping and splattering over the electric flat-top sending the scent of smoke and spices throughout the room—and placed it on the back burner to join her friend at the table. "I'm not sure we want to," Missy replied as she lifted Sondra's giant mug from the table, cupping it in her own delicate hands. "Well...we want to, but I think we'd like the surprise more. I mean, how often in life do you get to be *genuinely* surprised? I think it would make for such a beautiful moment. This smells *so* good."

She didn't drink Sondra's coffee as much as took in the aroma. Mocha. Her favorite. Caffeine was *no bueno* for the Fisher Guppy—Justin's coinage. As torturous as it was for Missy, she knew it was best for the health of the baby.

"You have such a good heart, Missy. You're going to make a wonderful mom."

Missy slid the cup across the table and fanned her face. "Stoooooop. You're going to make me cry! You know I'm hormonal."

Sondra reclaimed her coffee with one hand and patted Missy's arm with the other. "Honey, I hate to break it to you, but you're a sap *all the time*."

She winked, and Missy had to choke back the tears. "You hush. I am not." Total lie, of course.

Missy's mother Ines, Brazilian and stunningly beautiful (as was Missy), was wise to her daughter's sensitivity early on. In fact, she was convinced the only reason Missy cried upon delivery was because she somehow knew childbirth hurt, and felt bad for inflicting pain on her mother. Ines also attributed Missy's vegetarianism to this predisposed want to only aid and comfort. She seemed to know the proteins in front of her had come at something else's expense, something that could think and feel pain, and she wanted nothing to do with it. The bacon was for Justin.

She smiled again.

"You never did answer my question," Sondra said, gently slapping the table top to snap Missy from her stupor.

"What question?"

"What it is you two plan on doing about all this."

Missy's smile slipped some, but never quite fashioned into a frown. Only on the rarest of occasions could she find something to make her miserable enough to do so. But she did sigh. "Honestly? I don't know. We're not *totally* broke—Justin did use some disgrace—but I wanted to keep what we have left of Grands' money stashed away, just in case. With this economy…"

Missy trailed off on purpose. What she said wasn't a lie, but it also wasn't the whole truth. It was nice to have a cushion, but it was better to have a safety net—particularly if your fiancé was prone to falling.

"You know you can always come to me, right? If you need help?"

"I know. And I'm grateful. But really…we're going to be okay. It won't be easy, and it won't be quick, but Justin wants to change; he means to be better, and he's working hard to prove it. Whatever the solution, we'll find it. Together."

"Honey, I just hope you're not setting yourself up for disappointment—and I mean that in the nicest possible way. You know I love Justin as much as I love you, but addiction is a savage beast and difficult to slay. I would hate for you to get anything less than everything you hope for. That's all."

"I'm not afraid."

Missy sat back in the aluminum folding chair and clasped her hands over her budding belly. She spoke to the child in utero as much as to Sondra.

"I know Justin—I *know* him. He means to change, and he will. Nothing short of some cosmic event could stop things from working out for the better. I'm not afraid."

But Missy *was* afraid of one thing, and when she looked into her lap and saw it, there wasn't enough positive thinking or good will in the world to keep her from losing her cool. She jumped from her chair, simultaneously knocking it over, and launched Sondra's coffee mug into the air. The vessel slammed back down splashing dark liquid over the black and white checkerboard pattern and onto her friend's blue jeans. Sondra herself pushed back in a hurry, tipping her own chair as well.

"What! What happened?"

Sondra used both hands to shoo the excess java from her jeans, but her eyes remained fixed on Missy who, by now, was in full-blown seize mode. Her legs shuffled as if she were running in place, her hands swatting and slapping at her body—thighs, hips, stomach (she was more careful there but still spastic), chest, neck, and finally, her hair. She bent over and batted at her head like a schizo shaking the senseless out.

"Missy, *what?*"

Missy heard Sondra holler but wasn't quite ready to relax yet. She hopped away toward the center of the room and continued to rake her hands through her hair, though she had little of it, a pixie cut her style of choice.

"*Mesalina!*"

That did it. Missy's eyes shot up at the shout of her given name—sort of a Pavlov's dogs thing. The only person who called her Mesalina anymore was her father when he had his 'I-am-Daddy' pants on. "Huh?"

The stillness, however, was not to be. It took only seconds before the shimmying—and a string of *ewewew!*—to resume.

Eventually, Missy mellowed. Meanwhile, Sondra grabbed a dish towel and cleaned the coffee from the table, shaking her head. "Was that some sort of pregnancy-induced demon possession? Do we need a priest?"

Missy gave herself one last rub-down, stuck her tongue out in a gagging gesture and said, "It was a creepy crawler."

Sondra raised an eyebrow. "A creepy crawler?"

"A creepy crawler. One of those *unholy* things that has nine thousand legs and moves faster than...poop...through a goose. It was on me."

"A bug, you're saying? That was about a bug."

"They're gross! I can't relax when I see those things. One appears, vanishes a split second later, and I wait for it to turn up *on* me. Blech."

"They're a good thing, you know," Sondra reasoned. "When those are around, you won't find any ants or roaches or any other pests. They're basically nature's little exterminators. A good thing."

"If those things *cured cancer* they wouldn't be a good thing."

Missy took a plate from the cupboard, lined it with paper towels, and scooped the bacon on top. At one point, a mound of meat dangling in the air between the tongs, she turned back to Sondra.

"That was mean. I shouldn't have said that. I'm a terrible person."

Sondra chuckled as she pulled her black hooded sweatshirt over her pale blond hair, and straightened her short bangs once everything was in place. She took the bacon out of Missy's hand and hugged her tight. "You're not a terrible person. I don't think you could be if you tried. I love you. I'll see you tomorrow, 'kay?"

"I love *you*," Missy said, hugging her friend tighter. "And yes, I'll see you tomorrow. Thank you for not making fun of me."

"I would never...to your face!"

Then she cried *HUGS!* and hurried out, her face disappearing from the crack in the screen door. Cool, Tennessee springtime air fanned in behind her.

"Very funny," Missy shouted, knowing Sondra would hear. "You're evil!"

She went back to the bacon and mumbled to herself. "*I'm* evil, too, for cooking this bacon. Poor little piggy. If the animal gods demand restitution, take it from Justin's karmic stock."

And then…*CRASH!*

***

Fisher's stomach growled.

They should have been at least ten miles closer to home by now with Cooter warning him to slow down, you're goin' too darn fast! Not here, stuck with the old bastard, creeping up on God-knows-what on the side of the Interstate. His stomach churned. Hunger or nerves, something was not sitting well. Missy had said something on the phone earlier about bacon. Four years in and he still did not have the heart to tell her he preferred sausage.

With his head kept low and his senses on high, he followed the old man among the rocky outcroppings of the mountainside wall, stepping over shredded tires and heaps of garbage thrown from windows. "Damnit, Cooter, the buzzer's going off! We've only got 15 minutes before the rig shuts down, and we're stuck for the night!"

Cooter shushed him as they drew closer to the glowing red object. Somewhere close, water dripped and pooled into a roadside trench. The cool night air brushed past their faces, bringing to them the odor of scorched metal and…something else. Something peppery and sharp. *Like an unwashed arm pit*, Fisher thought, wincing.

Guided by the weak glow of flashlights, they approached.

Surrounded by thick, curled sheets of smoking metal at the bottom of the mountain floor lay a small, cylindrical tube no bigger than a can of tennis balls. Even after the crash, it remained smooth and unmarked. A crimson glow seemed to illuminate the tube itself; the red metal blushed with heat. The few twigs that had sunk into the blackened earth of the crater had turned to ash.

Fisher drew in a deep breath, keeping his distance.

"Well, I'll be damned," Cooter mumbled, shuffling closer. "I think that's one of them illegal aliens!"

Fisher exhaled loudly. "It's not a Mexican, Cooter. It's…" *What the hell* is *that thing?*

Without a word, Cooter snatched a long stick from the roadside and knelt down before the crater.

Fisher grabbed his shoulder. "What are you doing?"

"Gonna give it a poke, boy, to see what the funky hell this thing is."

"Do you think that's such a good idea?"

Cooter laughed dryly. "Boy, you don't get to be my age by being stupid. Back in the old days we used to poke road patties—you know, road kill—with sticks just for fun. But we also did it to make damn sure that whatever lay there was doornail-dead, so it didn't get back up and run into the road. I want to make sure whatever the hell this thing is has bit the dust, that way we can figure out what to do about it."

I just want to go home! Fisher wanted to scream.

Tongue jutting between his lips, Cooter leaned forward and, without hesitation, jabbed the tube with the stick three times.

Something shrieked.

The two jumped back, Cooter falling on his rear end, the end of his stick singed and smoking.

"What the hell was that!" Fisher yelled.

Cooter slapped a wet cough from his chest. "Damned if I know." His eyes grew wide in the red light. He pointed forward. "Look."

Slowly, Fisher shuffled forward to the crater.

A thin, white line of light appeared down the middle of the tube, and after several seconds of *pop*s and *click*s the tube cracked and split open, the two halves falling apart. Steam hissed from the opening and released more of that hot, peppery stink. The red glow dulled. Once it completely died, they both aimed their flashlights at the contents within.

Something long and green wriggled between the separate halves. Two small arms reached up, and two tiny, clawed hands gripped the sides.

Fisher dropped his flashlight when a small pair of eyes blinked back at him.

"Holy shit!" He jumped backwards, nearly tripping over his own feet. "Come on, Cooter! Let's go! I don't want to see any more of this."

But the old man's focus was on their find. "Say what? We can't just leave!"

"Screw it!" Fisher tapped at his pants pockets and silently cursed himself. "You stay here, and I'll go back to the rig and grab my cell, okay?"

Cooter didn't blink. "Sure…"

Without his flashlight, Fisher darted up the rocky incline and hopped into the cab. The buzzer demanded his attention, but all it received was a middle finger. He located his cell phone, jabbed the HOME button to wake it from sleep mode, and sighed. No bars. "Figures."

At the bottom of the hill, Cooter screamed.

Heart racing, Fisher leapt from the cab and hurried down the hill, gravel scattering with every step. In the darkness ahead, Cooter's outline flailed about, the beam of his flashlight swirling against the granite walls. Just as Fisher approached, the old man gurgled and collapsed. Fisher then grabbed his own flashlight, knelt down and grabbed the back of Cooter's head. The old man's eyes rolled into the back of his skull, showing only the whites. "Cooter! Cooter! Wake up, man! What happened?"

Something made Fisher turn. He aimed the flashlight into the crater.

The tube was empty.

Panicked, Fisher jabbed the flashlight in all directions finding nothing but an empty interstate. "Cooter, man, come on, wake up," he said, not sure why he was suddenly whispering. When he only responded with another wet gurgle Fisher pulled Cooter to his feet and held him up under his arms. Thankfully, the old pervert didn't weigh much.

Fisher struggled, but managed to drag the two of them up the hill and situated Cooter back into the passenger seat. Fisher buckled him in and got back behind the wheel. The rig started up easily, but the trip back down would be anything but. Carefully, he dropped the truck into reverse and slowly—*very* slowly—backed it down the hill. He was terrified a smaller vehicle would come around the bend and crash into the trailer, but no one did.

Once they pulled back onto the interstate, Fisher guided the truck into the far right lane, finally letting himself breathe. But he was far from calm. Something was seriously wrong with Cooter, and the rig, no matter how fast he drove he only had five more minutes before it would shut off and remain inoperable for the next eight hours. He had to get the old man to a hospital quick, but he wasn't sure Monteagle even had one. His thoughts kept going back to the red metal tube…and the green worm-like *thing* squirming within. It was gone when he came back, so where did it…

Fisher turned toward Cooter.

Cooter's wide eyes were locked on his as something large ballooned in his throat.

***

Missy hauled butt into the living room, from which the commotion seemed to come.

Easily startled and already on pins and needles, she jogged through the narrow hall and into the gloom of their living room, bacon-greased tongs still in hand. With only one window and little to go off but moonlight, Missy focused hard, not only on finding the source of the noise but remembering what it was in the first place.

Did books fall off the shelf? Did glass break?

She used her free hand to feel along the wall for the light switch behind her, but her eyes continued to search the room. She could make out more of the rectangular recesses in the wall serving as her book shelves—Justin wasn't much of a reader—but nothing appeared out of place. The glass of the window remained intact, so that wasn't it. Missy eventually found the switch, flipped it, and the floor lamp in the back corner, opposite the books, filled the space with soft amber light.

The search was over.

On the floor behind the futon was Missy's aloe plant, overturned. A few of the thick, fleshy leaves had snapped and oozed their soothing fluid onto her no longer spotless carpet. Dirt spilled over the decorative clay pot and spread out like filthy tendrils. Little brown paw-print shaped smudges led away from the plant and out the way she'd come.

"Ugh! Flippin' cat! Puss, where are you?"

She did a quick search of the room, but there weren't too many places for the pain in the rump to hide.

"Pussface!"

She didn't expect the cat to respond but bent down on all fours to check beneath the sofa, careful not to grind *more* soil into the carpet. She thought she heard something, a rustling, but assumed it was her weight on the futon as she went down. Missy put her face in the space between the couch and the floor and…

Nothing.

Stupid cat was stupid *and* M.I.A.

Missy sighed, sat back on her legs and set to scooping up her spilt potted plant.

She turned it upright, pouting as she fingered the broken leaves, then set the tongs on the table from which it had fallen—she'd need both hands to scoop up the excess dirt. The soil cooled her hands and warmed her heart, one of Missy's favorite sensations. It reminded her of her mother and the times they'd spent in her backyard garden.

The first handful, aerated and silky, she fiddled with a bit before returning it to the pot, more lost in thought than anything. But when she did actually <u>look</u> at the second handful...she wanted to be sick all over it.

Squirming throughout the soil were at least two of the same horrid bugs she'd earlier found nesting in her lap.

Their eighteen-thousand legs wriggled as the creatures tunneled in and out of sight, above the dirt and below it. Long antennae stuck straight up off their heads—*two, like devil horns, because they're evil*—and whirled through the air as if to draw in and feed off Missy's discomfort. Not wanting to, but forcing herself to do so, Missy looked down at the mess on the floor.

More bugs.

Two, three…ten? It didn't matter. And there were more still in the plant itself, a couple slinking out over the edge and scurrying out of sight.

All this happened in a matter of seconds but, after what felt like an eon, she flung the contents of her hands as far from herself as possible and dashed, still on hands and knees, for the doorway.

She'd almost made it through before Puss barreled into the room, zipping right under and straight through her arms and legs like she'd never been there at all.

"What the—?"

Missy put her head down and watched between her knees and upside down as the cat wigged out on the other side of the room. He darted from one spot to the next, shook his head and kicked his legs out, sometimes lying down and rolling over, and ground his head into the carpet before doing it all over again.

"Pudder…"

She forgot all about the bugs. The cat was upset, which made *her* upset. Missy pulled herself up and approached the tabby.

"Pussface…Pudder…what's up, buddy? What's got you spooked?"

The poor, stupid beast was still tweaked but he calmed a bit when he saw Missy coming. He sat down but wouldn't stop jerking his head to the side, pawing at his ear.

"Come here, fat boy. Let me see."

Missy scratched Puss's opposite ear to soothe him while she checked the one giving him grief. She folded his dark ear back and, at first, thought there was a wad of hair stuck in there, which would explain his irritation. It must have itched like crazy. Then she watched the wad unfold…unfurl…and crawl out of the animals ear drum and down his white fur throat.

Missy hollered and jumped back. Pussface shook himself and ran out into the hall.

"That's it!" she cried, waving her hands as if she'd burned them. "I've had it! Where's my phone?"

She knew Justin couldn't do anything about it at the moment, but she was starting to get a complex, and she could at least whine to someone other than the cat. Missy hopped the stairs two at a time to retrieve her phone from the bedroom.

She found her trusty old clam-shell phone on the night stand and dialed Justin's number as she continued to dry-heave and shoo imaginary bugs from her body. "Come on, boy, answer the phone." Missy bounced impatiently and counted the rings—two, three, four. Justin answered on the fifth ring, but he barely got through *Missy!* before she shrieked.

"You need to come home! And take me to a hotel! No way I'm staying here...*ugh!*"

There was a lot of interference on Justin's end. She had a hard time making out what he said.

"Justin? Can you hear me? Are you almost home? I'm bugging out!"

Missy smacked herself in the forehead for the ridiculous pun.

"They were on me, Justin," she whined. "They had legs and intentions."

She thought she heard someone cry out in the background, heard Justin yell, but again, the interference. "Justin!"

Call dropped.

She dialed his number again, but it went straight to voicemail.

"Perfect! Lovely! Just me and the stupid cat in a house full of scuttling parasites."

The words resonated, echoed off the walls of her mind. *A house full of scuttling parasites...*

"A house full?"

Missy caught her reflection in the mirror atop the dresser.

It moved.

Or rather, things moved *over* it.

"Justin," she whispered. "Please come home."

***

The truck shut off as they rolled into the parking lot of the crowded rest area. Fisher carefully glided the rig into the last free spot in the back of the lot and shifted it into park. The engine sighed, but Fisher found he could not do the same.

He quickly unbuckled and crawled over to Cooter. He reached out to touch him, but something stopped him. The massive bulge in the old man's throat had—thankfully—receded and disappeared, but Fisher still felt uneasy, helpless. The old man lay motionless in his seat, other than his eyes rolling in his head like bowling balls down a lane.

"Cooter! Come on, you old fuck, say something!" Now that he was this close, he noticed something was very off. Cooter's skin appeared splotchy and gray, and speckled with flecks of black. And was that smoke drifting out from between his teeth?

The black spots grew larger.

Fisher panicked.

The nearest hospital could be miles away, and the rig—the Goddamn rig!—was dead for the next eight hours. "Seriously, Cooter, say something—anything!"

Cooter's body jerked and tensed up. His fingers curled over the edge of the arm rests. Smoke seeped from his fingertips.

The overhead light snapped on as the passenger door clicked and swung open. An obese woman wearing little more than a tube top and fishnets stepped up into the cab and grinned a jagged smile. Her massive breasts jiggled. "Heya, boys! Either of you two manly men lookin' fo a little slap 'n tickle?"

Lot lizard.

"Get lost," Fisher growled.

The woman turned toward Cooter. "Coota! Ya old fart! I haven't seen ya in a dog's age. Why haven't ya been visiting with dear ol' Mama Gracie?"

Cooter hitched and coughed, exhaling a thick cloud of smoke.

She bent forward, eyes narrowed. "What's wrong with him?" She slapped Fisher's shoulder.

"Nothing, he's just a little sick right now—bad gas station hot dog. Look, just leave us—"

Another lot lizard appeared behind Mama Gracie, this one more petite. "Cooter! Well, I'll be damned!"

Fisher tried to reason. "Ladies, listen, Cooter is very sick right now. I need to get him to a hospital."

Mama Gracie unbuckled Cooter and lifted him from his seat like a child. "I'll tell ya what, string bean. I'll take care of sweet ol' Coota here. I'm all this ol' man needs."

"No, no, no!" Fisher exited the cab and met her on the other side. "Please, just put him back. I need to find—"

The smaller lizard stepped up to him and jabbed the business end of a switch blade to his neck, stopping Fisher dead.

"Ya best jus' let Mama do her magic, string bean. Maybe I'll letcha have a crack at *this* crack later!" The girl licked her lips and smiled, revealing a mouth absent of teeth. She lowered the knife, blew him a kiss and took off after Mama and Cooter.

"Jesus..." Fisher sighed. "Could this night get any worse?"

Fisher reluctantly followed the two hookers and his work mate into the brightly lit welcome center, then into the men's restroom. An old security guard slept soundlessly at his desk in a small room across the hall. The two women giggled and cooed, whispering charming obscenities to Cooter as they carried him into the handicap stall and closed the door behind them.

Drained, Fisher collapsed onto the tiled bathroom floor—*It looks clean enough*, he thought—and closed his eyes. In his mind's eye he could still see the bright flash, the near collision, the tube...the thing inside. Fisher curled into himself and shivered violently. It wasn't that he was cold; he had finally snapped. His body couldn't handle anymore. The day was done. He was supposed to be back home by now, hugging his fiancé, petting his cat, eating his stupid bacon. Instead, he was sitting on the floor of a rest area bathroom while two hookers gave Cooter a full service check under his hood.

Fisher nearly screamed when his phone vibrated. He pulled his cell from his pocket and stared at it for a minute before finally snapping it open.

"Missy!"

"*shhhhhhhhhh*…need…*shhhhhhh*…hotel! And…*shhhhhhhhh*…staying here…"

The static and interference was so thick he could only make out every other word.

"Missy? Missy, can you hear me?"

"*shhhhhhhhhhh*... they were on me!"

From inside the stall, the two hookers screamed. Fisher dropped his cell phone. The back cover snapped, sending the battery skipping across the floor.

The hookers continued to shriek, long and hard, as they threw themselves against the thin metal walls of the stall. Smoke plumed and filled the corner of the room. Fisher leaned over and peered under the door.

An explosion rocked the small restroom, throwing Fisher clear to the other side. His back hit the far wall near the door before he crumpled like a wet blanket. Fisher sat up, groaned at the throbbing in his side and tried to stand. The billows of smoke lifted and expired as quickly as they'd come.

The hookers had stopped screaming.

"Cooter?" he coughed.

Fisher took a step forward, but stopped when the door to the stall swung open.

The remnants of smoke separated as Cooter—or what he had become—*slithered* through the doorway.

***

I've had it up to my tits with this.

Missy'd heard Sondra say it a million times and, while she herself couldn't form the words, she could appreciate them now, particularly if things continued on this way, then there would be enough of the disgusting beasts to do so.

There were almost more bugs on the mirror than glass, and dozens of others coming out of the woodwork. Literally. They crept out of holes in the baseboards she didn't even know were there, through windowsills, from under the closet door. But the final straw came when Missy found some scurrying out of the corner of her underwear drawer. The thought of those things going anywhere *near* her unmentionables, whether on her body at the time or not, made her tingle in a most unwanted way.

"You are *totally* uninvited, here," she said before running out the door.

Missy stood in the hall and ruffled her hair out of sheer blankness. She was confused, freaked out, agitated, and concerned about her fiancé and didn't know which issue to tackle first. But, as was often the case in stressful situations, biology took over…and told her she had to pee.

Missy skipped a few feet down the hall and into the tiny bathroom, not bothering to hit the switch before sitting on the toilet—the faux candle in the window provided enough illumination for her to do what she needed to do.

Not a moment passed after she heard the first tinkle before she saw the first creeper.

It had come from beneath the shelves not three feet from her. Pants around her ankles and heart in her throat, Missy did the first thing that came to her, which was to grab a bottle of bathroom cleaner beneath the sink. She was still…*going*…and therefore unable to run, so this seemed like the next best solution. Missy twisted her legs as far away from the bug—the *big* bug—as they would go and fired.

The beast was at least as thick as her thumb and too angry to die because no matter how many times she sprayed, it kept coming. And the closer it came, the louder Missy cried out. "*Gitgitgit!*"

The room reeked of noxious fumes and made Missy's eyes tear—at least, that's what she told herself. The bug had become a walking chemical cloud, a trail of white foam left in its wake. Its progress slowed, but not enough for her liking, so she put the nozzle as close to the insect as possible and pumped...and didn't stop pumping until she blew the thing back into the corner, watching it like a hawk to make sure it moved no more.

When it didn't, Missy slipped her bottoms back on and went for the hand sanitizer—and found more bugs. The sanitizer, the faucet, the whole basin was crawling with them, all slinking up through the drain. Missy jumped back and almost fell into the tub but managed to grab the shower curtain in time, ripping it away from a few of the hooks to reveal a swarm within. Body wash, soap dish, the shower caddy with her toothbrush and toothpaste on it...not one surface went untouched by their filthy little legs. She could actually *hear* their rigid, wretched bodies rubbing against one another, an obscene whispering.

Missy gagged and made a break for the stairs but stopped at the landing. So far she'd seen the crawlers in every room of the house, but there was still one space she hadn't checked. Missy put one hand on her belly and another over her mouth, palm out, nauseated by something other than the pregnancy. She *really* didn't want to check this room because part of her knew what she would find, and knew how upset, how *angry* she was going to be if the room had been violated by these revolting creatures. She sighed.

"Just open the door, Missy."

So she did.

And found her infant's nursery teeming with creeping life.

The soft green walls were crisscrossed with trails of them, not quite as organized as an ant march but following something reminiscent of a route. The white furniture was spotted with their wicked little bodies, light from the baby zoo animal lamp muted by the sheer amount of bugs amassed on the shade. And the crib… The *crib*. The green and purple pastel quilt Missy had loved so much was wholly concealed under the cover of the multi-legged cockroaches. The doe-eyed lion and the happy hippo she found so endearing were erased, her baby's haven, erased, and with it, Missy's patience.

She stomped her feet in the doorway and snarled.

"Soil our Guppy's room, will you? God help you, beasties, 'cause I sure won't."

Missy took one step into the hall and was body-checked.

***

The restroom door swung open and the old security guard from the lobby ran in, halting when he eyed the monstrosity slinking through the stall door.

"What in tarnations!"

Fisher quickly shuffled backwards, away from the bloated, gray membrane Cooter had become, and stood behind the old man. The creature groaned and jiggled as two humanlike arms and legs stretched from its jellylike body and lifted its bulk upright, though its torso remained a shapeless blob that trailed behind it like a coattail. Its face altered and rearranged until it formed something resembling the old man with which he'd once shared his work duties.

Of all the things Fisher could have thought at that particular moment, the only thing to hit him was, *Mr. Coscom is going to be so pissed...*

The security guard looked beyond Cooter to the smoking piles of lot lizard gore staining the handicapped stall. "My God..."

In the time it took to blink, Cooter's bloated arm shot out and stretched across the room, attaching itself to the old security guard's face. Smoke billowed from the man's head, filling the room with the stink of cooked meat and burnt hair. He barely had time to scream before his entire body inflated and burst, showering

Fisher in a chunky, liquid red nightmare. The creature retracted its arm and hissed.

Fisher threw open the door and broke into a sprint through the empty lobby, shouldering open the front doors.

He collided with several truckers standing at the entrance.

The one in front, who sported a jean jacket and golden, waistline mullet, grabbed Fisher by his shirt to stop him. "Whoa there, young buck!"

"Let me go!" Fisher struggled against his grip.

"Hold on a second. What the shit was that explosion a minute ago?"

Another trucker with a large gut spit a wad of tobacco on the sidewalk. "Yeah? You wasn't droppin' M-80s in the john, now was ya'? Kids come through here all the time to do stupid shit like that and blame it on us."

The remaining truckers nodded. "Yeah!"

Mullet glanced over Fisher's shoulder, his eyes wide. "What the shit?"

The lobby exploded into a mess of glass and metal as Cooter streamed through the front of the building as if it were not there. It appeared bigger now, its massive bulk swaying back and forth like Jello shaking on a plate. Mullet loosened his grip, and Fisher rolled out of the way before Cooter got any closer. After making it to the edge of the parking lot, curiosity got the better of him. He stopped to look over his shoulder.

The truckers screamed and turned to run, but Cooter shot several more long, gray appendages their way, attaching themselves to the men and freezing them in place. Instantly, they became pillars of smoke and, soon after, steaming heaps of their former selves. Blood and various body parts showered the front lawn. Fisher gazed on in a sick fascination as Cooter grew larger, becoming nearly as tall as the building itself.

Fisher kept low and weaved between the rows of trucks, doing his best to lose the creature following him. He ducked under the truck trailers near the back of the lot, checking every door handle as they came along. But he struggled with keeping quiet—his clothes were blood soaked, and his breath was nowhere to be found, each one more of a struggle than the last. Every cell in his body told him to scream, to rid his mind of the impossibilities he had witnessed, but he knew he couldn't. He had too much to live for. He had only just started to regain Missy's trust (but with someone as overly nice as her, it was not difficult), and with their little guppy on the way... There was no chance he was going to watch its first steps from the afterlife.

Fisher jerked stiff when he heard something slide across the driveway. He slapped a hand over his mouth and slowly knelt down to peek under the rigs. Nothing. He checked a few more cabs before finally finding one unlocked. He quietly opened the door and slipped inside, ignoring the stale reek of marijuana and sweat. From that high up he could see over the hoods of several other cabs to the front of the building, where the remains of the truckers cooled in the night air. But no sign of Cooter.

Fisher searched the cab for a set of keys, silently hoping they weren't in someone's current possession. He popped open the glove compartment and was surprised to find a very shiny, very large Magnum revolver. He had heard of truckers carrying guns before, but had yet to encounter anyone who cared, for obvious reasons, to admit to it. Fisher snatched the gun, finding it fully loaded, and closed the compartment.

He looked down and sighed, feeling a bit stupid. The keys were still in the ignition. Hands sweating, he gripped the key and turned, praying the truck wasn't dead for the night. The rig purred to life, and the alarm remained silent. *There are some miracles still left in this world*, he thought. He caught his breath and shifted the cab into drive, letting the truck and its attached trailer slowly roll out of its space. Then he thought, *Screw it*, and jammed down the accelerator. *I've got the truck now, and I've got the gun!*

But his thoughts changed immediately when he turned right, toward the exit. Cooter towered over the last row of trucks, its girth nearly covering the entire exit ramp. It held several more unfortunate truckers in place while it proceeded to turn them inside-out. His fear gone, and gun in hand, Fisher floored the accelerator and drove straight toward it.

Cooter's massive bulk turned to face Fisher as he closed in.

The truck smashed directly into it, which threw Fisher against the steering wheel. His face hit the dashboard, and his mouth filled with blood as his two front teeth flew from his mouth. He was frightened the monstrosity would stop the truck and, for the moment, it did. Cooter's gray, distorted face filled the windshield and moved closer until its arm-sized lips pressed against the glass.

"*Fiiiiiisssshhhheeeeeeer.*"

Fisher lifted the gun and pulled the trigger three times.

Cooter squealed and toppled backwards onto the pavement. Black blood splashed over the hood and through the open windshield. Fisher retched as it sprayed across his face and into his mouth, the foul taste rolling over his tongue and down his throat. He coughed up a puff of smoke. But there was no time to waste. He took his free moment and kicked the accelerator, pinning the creature to the ground as he drove right over it. The truck jostled and shook violently before hitting ground and continuing onto the interstate.

He kept his eyes on the road, focusing with every fiber of his being to make it home without crashing.

Fifteen miles, baby, and I'll be there!

Smoke poured out from the bottom of the cab.

***

Missy screamed and brought her hands up to protect her face, though she had already been knocked across the hall.

"It's just me, Missy! It's Sondra! Are you okay?"

Missy gritted her teeth and scowled at her friend. "Are you *bonkers?* You almost gave me a heart attack!"

"I'm sorry! I called you from the kitchen, but I guess you didn't hear. I didn't see you come out of there until it was too late. *Are you okay?* Tell me I didn't hit your stomach."

Missy grabbed her tiny hips and leaned against the wall, shaking her head. "No, hon, I'm fine. You just scared me, is all. What are you doing here, anyway?"

"Stupid me. I was on my way to the gallery when I realized I'd left my camera. I think I had it in the living room last?"

Missy nodded and tried to manage her harried nerves. "It should still be there."

"'Kay. I hate to hit and run but I have Neal waiting in the car. You sure you're all right? You looked razzed."

"*That* is an understatement."

"What's wrong?"

Missy told Sondra what had happened since she left—the cat, the bugs, and worst of all, not being able to reach Justin, not knowing if or when he would come home. She almost started to cry when she heard the rumble of a rig out front, followed by Justin's tell-tale honk.

It started as a joke at Missy's expense. He'd caught her watching *The Little Mermaid* videos online one morning, and thought it'd be funny to beep—as best he could—the tune to one of the songs when he got home that night. He'd never intended it to stick, he told her, but she'd taken such enjoyment from it he couldn't bring himself to stop.

Missy breathed a big sigh of relief. "Thank God."

Sondra started to say something but was cut off by a ruckus outside. "What was *that?*"

Missy shook her head in confusion and listened. Metal. Grinding. *A car accident?* Some kind of…*hissing*...like air escaping. *Did a hose on the truck blow?* And a man. Shouting. She couldn't make out what. "Neal?"

Sondra shrugged.

Concerned, both women made for the stairs when a tremendous crash rocked the house. *An earthquake!* The walls rumbled and the floor shook, knocking both Missy and Sondra on their keisters. Sondra recovered quickly and got onto her hands and knees, while Missy stared at the ceiling to make sure it wasn't crumbling over their heads.

Moments went by before the din dissipated, the splintering wood and shattering glass thinning out, quieting, like the last few kernels of corn popping in the bag.

"Was that a *bomb*?" Sondra whispered.

"Who would want to bomb Chattanooga?"

"Someone who missed Nashville." Sondra shook and rose to her feet. "I'll go find out. Stay here."

"No, Sondra! I'll come with you."

Before Missy could move, Sondra shot out a finger and pointed at her belly. *You're pregnant, idiot*, her stern face said. *Stay.* She nodded and sat cross-legged in the center of the hall, watching her friend disappear down the stairwell, amazed she hadn't started to cry.

There was a clatter in the front yard.

Sondra screamed.

Missy shot upright. "*Sondra!*"

"Missy!" her friend cried. "Stay. Up. Stairs!"

Sondra appeared on the landing, her face void of all color, tears streaming. She grabbed Missy's hand and bawled. "We have to go! Is there a fire escape? A landing we could jump from a window down onto? I know it's dangerous for you, honey, but we don't have a choice."

Missy cried. "I don't understand! Where's Justin?"

"Right here, baby girl!"

He's hurt, Missy thought. But he was coming up the stairs, which she assumed was a good sign, so she went for him. "Justin!"

"*NO!*"

Sondra snatched her up, almost pulling Missy's arm from her shoulder. "Ow! Sondra…"

"Something's wrong with him, Missy! He's not—"

"*What's wrong with him?*" *Oh, God*, she begged. *Please don't take him from me. Not him. I couldn't bear it.* "Sondra, let me go!"

"Let her go, Sondra. Gonna getchas, anyway."

Missy stopped wrestling and stiffened, Sondra's warning sinking in. *Something's wrong with him.* She heard it in his voice and mistook it for injury, but hearing him now, listening to what he said, *how* he said it, he wasn't just hurt. He was…altered. His speech made her woozy. But before she could think of falling down, Justin bumbled into the crowded hall.

Or at least, something resembling Justin did.

Missy could hardly *begin* to process the nature of the creature swaying before her.

She *could* understand why he had trouble balancing, ambling—he had no feet to speak of. A tan boot was still on the end of one leg but something oozed through the eyelets, out over the top, and down the laces. The other 'foot' was just a long...*tentacle?*...poking out of the pant-leg and dragging behind him.

His abdomen was distended, more of the gelatinous substance pushed through his flannel shirt, the buttons about to snap. His throat was swollen, and his head appeared misshapen, though it was hard to tell with the giant Native American headdress hanging over it.

The headdress was more surreal but certainly not the *worst* part of Justin's appearance.

Missy put a hand over her belly.

Sondra put hers over Missy's, gently shooing Missy behind her.

Missy meant to run, *wanted* to run, but all she could do was press herself against the hallway wall, never taking her eyes off what she hoped, even now, could still be her fiancé. Sondra stayed close.

"Cooter blood," Justin gurgled. "Tube funk. WOO!"

Sondra wept as Justin lifted the amorphous mass of what could no longer pass as a human arm into the air, her little brother's head dangling from it.

"For Guppy!" Justin squealed. "A mobile. Spinny!"

He batted it with a semi-humanoid hand, and Neal's head made a few dizzying rotations before his hair tightened up, forcing it to spin in the opposite direction. Sondra sobbed louder.

"What have you done?" Missy whimpered.

"Gonna getchas, babies," Justin tittered, forming a grisly smile. "Gonna getchas. But first…"

Justin held the head high and raised his booted foot, taking a most flamboyant step. When he did so with the other gooey appendage, the slopping made Missy teeter on the edge of sanity.

She didn't understand what he was doing at first, why he walked that way, but once he seemed more used to the movement and could keep himself from wobbling, she figured it out.

It was an awful masquerade, a shameful, alien imitation of an Indian marching.

He looked like something you'd find in a tasteless cartoon, bumbling down the hall, chanting, feathers on the headdress swaying—an embarrassing stereotype.

But in his current state, he was nothing short of terrifying.

His eyes were absolutely wild, rolling about in his head like nothing kept them in place. And Missy was almost certain he was…changing…before her very eyes. He seemed to take up more and more space in the hall as he progressed. And the smell, the *reek* of corruption…

Missy covered her mouth with both hands, tears pouring down over her fingers. Sondra, back also to the wall, still kept an arm stretched over Missy's belly. Both women's eyes were *wide* open, fixed on the perversion of this friend, this lover, as it did its macabre dance.

When it reached the end of the hall and could go no further, it stopped, shook, and more of Justin disappeared with each passing second.

Missy looked away, unable to take anymore, when something screeched on the stairs. The light from the downstairs hall was swallowed by a *second* glutinous mass, this one took up every inch of space in the stairwell. Smoke and slickened tendrils crept up over the landing.

"Cooter," Justin garbled, his human voice almost non-existent.

Missy grabbed Sondra's hand, held it tight, when something tickled her foot.

For an agonizing moment, she thought for sure one of the blob's slimy appendages had wrapped itself around her ankle and was about to suck her into itself. But when she looked down...

Bugs. Everywhere.

She'd forgotten all about them.

Missy breathed hard and watched as they poured through every doorway, grazed her and Sondra's feet, clearly in a hurry to get where they were going...and they appeared to going for her fiancé and his former co-worker.

Missy watched in horror as hundreds, *thousands* of insects swarmed out of the rooms and into her living nightmare. She couldn't believe this many of the animals existed *anywhere* on earth, let alone in her home, as she watched them envelop both Justin and Cooter in seconds.

She could hear them cry out beneath—the creatures, *blobs*; she could hear them snarl in what she assumed was protest—but just barely. The swishing and scraping of the throng of pests she had cursed not thirty minutes ago, now seemed to be saving her, her friend, and her infant's lives, it was too great to ignore.

But she had to try.

Missy covered her ears, curled in on herself, and stayed that way—*Minutes? Hours?*—until she felt a hand brush through her hair. "It's done, sweetie."

Missy sniffed some of the snot she knew ran from her nose and looked up at Sondra.

"It's done."

Her first thought was often her only thought.

Justin.

She twisted around Sondra and found what she had expected: nothing but tattered garments.

Missy's mind diverted around this sad, miserable truth and steered her elsewhere, forced her to say something that would have been funny under difference circumstances. Anesthetized, staring at the back wall, she said, "He had a headdress."

"Neal was wearing it." Her friend sounded just as numb. "We were taking it back to the gallery."

"Hmm."

Missy crawled across the hall and sat against the wall, facing Sondra.

They appeared to be the only life-forms left.

"See?" Sondra said, wiping a tear from her cheek. "What'd I say? You have these bugs…but no pests."

Missy leaned over and upchucked.

Story Notes

We had an absolute blast writing this story. I'm a huge Edward Lee fan, I wanted this to be my little tribute to the gross-out master. I wasn't sure what to expect when we started it. I wrote the Fisher and Cooter stuff, and Nikki worked on Missy and Sondra. I had a lot of fun playing off her sections, and I hope to do more co-writing in the future. By the way, if you haven't ever traveled south down I-24 through Monteagle in Tennessee into Chattanooga, it's a little scary. It's a hell of a down-grade through the mountains, but the countryside is gorgeous. If you do, go check out Rock City and Ruby Falls. They're pretty neat.

CONFUSION IN SOUTHERN ILLINOIS

Pat heard Georgie crying. He huffed and stood up from the couch, dropping his newspaper, before stomping to the hallway. *Damn Georgie*, he thought, *and damn house.* It was always so cold in this rickety old house, even in the summer. The crisp air bit through his slippers.

Georgie immediately perked at the sight of Pat, then turned to the wall and whined. He shuffled where he sat, looking at the wall then back at Pat.

"What is it, boy?" Pat scratched him under the chin. Georgie would need a shave soon. He was getting a bit mangy.

Georgie backed up and revealed a small, wide open door set low on the wall.

Pat sighed, "Did you drop your ball down the laundry chute again?"

Georgie barked into the open hole.

"Damn it." Pat opened the door to the basement, then took the stairs carefully, one at a time. The house was easily over a hundred years old, so there was no reason to get cocky, trip, and fall to his death, especially so soon after inheriting it from his grandparents. It was a terrible circumstance, being raised by his grandparents after his parents both died, only to see them slowly slip into senility. Then there was the dementia. That was a whole other thing.

No matter. The house was his now. *Not* theirs.

The basement still gave him that same old shiver. It was so creepy, and it always reminded him of the cellar from *Evil Dead*. Canned vegetables shelved in the back corner, gourds hanging on strings from the ceiling. He was amazed, even now, that some nightmarish creature didn't live down here, feeding off his childish insecurities.

He searched by the light of the basement window.

There, in the far corner, was Georgie's squeaky ball. Pat quickly crossed the basement and reached down to grab the toy when a skinny arm reached out and snatched his wrist. Pat nearly yelped.

"Where…am I?" a frail voice asked. Jolie crawled out from the dark corner on all fours. Her bluish white hair was knotted and plastered over her wrinkled face.

"No no, Grandma Jolie," Pat said. "You need to be a good kitty and go back to your corner."

"P-Pat? Is…what…" She stared up at him with pale blue eyes. A rare moment of clarity. "Pat? Where am I? So…hungry."

This just won't do. Pat leaned down and smacked the old woman across the face.

"Stop it! You know better! Cats don't talk."

"But—"

Another smack.

He leaned in closer. "Meow."

At first Jolie looked confused, but her eyes slowly clouded over, and her head waved.

"Meow," he said.

"Me...meow," she replied.

Pat snatched up the ball and watched Grandma crawl back to her dark corner like a good kitty. Maybe, when she was further along and less a liability, she could come back upstairs with Georgie. He looked up the laundry chute at Grandpa's face.

"Got your ball."

Georgie barked back happily.

Story Notes

I really love the idea of hiding something in plain sight. Originally, I wasn't sure if I wanted to go a little silly with this story, as it easily could have been, but I decided to play it completely straight. The house and the basement itself was taken from my great grandmother's house in rural Illinois, and it's the only house I've ever been to with a laundry chute in the wall. Her basement always creeped me out. I went back recently to visit and even as an adult I still have a hard time checking it out. There's all kinds of weird stuff down there, gourds hanging from the ceiling, an old loom, numerous jars of God-knows-what in the corner, a dark room in the back I've always refused to go near...

KING CAKE

Olivia was greeted at the front door by Cain, her sister's uptight husband, and the cacophony of all five of their snarling little girls. The house was far too warm, always too loud, and a little like walking into a Chuck E. Cheese on report card day. Of all days, it was the absolute last thing she wanted to do.

Cain welcomed her with a hug and quick peck on the cheek, and guided her into the dining room where she found her brother Ronnie and her sister Marla and her husband. She exchanged pleasantries and plopped down next to her brother's boyfriend Jamal.

Beaming, her eldest sister Sam welcomed them with pan-roasted lemon chicken and potatoes au gratin; the same dull routine every month. It was Sam's idea, these prescheduled sibling get-togethers, and it was to honor their late mother's request to stay close as a family unit and to be reminded that all they had was each other.

What a crock of shit, Olivia thought sourly.

Instead of simply eating their overcooked chicken and catching up, the meals typically ended in hurt feelings and people awkwardly rushing to get their coats. Sam had not always been the easiest to get along with.

Unlike the other two, growing up with Sam was like living with a forty-year-old spinster: dour and in desperate need of direction. Heart disease took their father not long after Olivia was born, and Sam and their mother turned to church for comfort. Both were constantly pushing their religion and family values onto her siblings, starting in on her before she could even walk. Mother desperately wanted the family name to live on, and Sam was damn determined to oblige, even if the others wouldn't. Sam was pregnant with her first two before she hit nineteen…neither of which belonged to Cain. Her other three siblings continued to live life however the hell they saw fit.

Olivia was itching to leave the moment her fork hit her empty plate. Cain quickly cleared the table off and retreated to the kitchen.

"God bless our family, young and old," Sam said, standing with her hands in the air. "We come here every month in honor of our late mother: our caretaker, our birthing vessel, our light in our darkest times."

Groaning, Olivia shifted in her seat. *Her* only prayer was to let this horseshittery end quickly.

"Mother was there for us when we needed her most, and…I was there for her in her last few days of precious life, helping to usher her off to meet our Lord and maker so that they may be together forever. We love her and miss her. God bless her unfettered spirit, and God bless us, her wondrous creations. Amen."

A collective sigh from the rest of the table.

Marla retorted, "Must we go through this every damn month, Sam? I cannot stress to you how sorry I am that I wasn't able to be with Mom when she passed. Victor and I had business with our company outside of the country. We had no choice." Her husband nodded solemnly.

Sam turned her head away, frowning. She eyed her brother.

"Don't look at me," Ronnie said. "Mother never exactly approved of my lifestyle." He caressed Jamal's hand and kissed the back of it.

Olivia blurted, "This is bullshit, Sam! I'm tired of these stupid ass dinners and fake remembrances. It's been a year. Can't we just place some daisies on her fucking grave from now on and maybe only see each other on birthdays?"

Sam grimaced. "Don't you *dare* use that language in my house, Olivia! I already allow you in my home— you, a stripper—with those hideous tattoos and facial piercings and loose morals, but foul words will *not* be permitted!" She glanced into the living room as her children ate and screamed wildly at their plastic Sesame Street folding table.

"Fucking please," Olivia said. "My foul language seems to be a problem, but our letting our brother prance around with his faggy boyfriend in front of your kids isn't? No offense, boys." She blew them a kiss.

They both laughed and caught her affection in mid-air. "None taken, bitch."

"Enough!" Sam roared. The table went quiet, as did her children. "This is supposed to be a happy occasion. To celebrate our mother's life and love for us. She wanted us to adore one another and carry on her spirit. As you can see, I've already complied with her requests."

"Yeah, five times and counting," Ronnie giggled.

Sam grinned. "Counting indeed." She rubbed her stomach.

"Get out of here, Sam," said Marla. "Again?"

Sam nodded happily.

"Cain *has* heard of the pull out method, right?" asked Olivia. "I'm sure you've got a church bush big enough to catch it all."

The whole table laughed.

Sam continued to smirk. "Today, more than any other, is a special day. Today we all get to share in my celebration. Cain?"

From out of the kitchen, Sam's husband carried a large baking pan, which he gingerly placed on the table for everyone to see. In the pan was a large circular cake, its golden baked dough carefully braided like a little girl's hair. Dusted across the white frosted glaze were numerous festive candy colors of purples, yellows and greens. The smell instantly lit up the room.

Ronnie asked, "Is that—"

"A King Cake?" Sam finished. "Yes, it is. Straight from Louisiana. Our friend Alexandrine DeBaillion owns a wonderful bakery in New Orleans. I had him specially make this one and ship it to us."

Marla clapped her hands. "I've heard of these! Isn't there supposed to be, like, a small plastic baby baked inside, and whoever gets it in their slice is the next to…have a…" She frowned and wilted in her seat. Victor rubbed her shoulders.

"Ooooh, girl, at least we ain't got to worry about that," Ronnie giggled to Jamal.

Olivia's mouth watered. A warm, cinnamon aroma permeated the air. Cain cut them each a hefty slice, but he and Sam did not imbibe. Everyone moaned as they dug in.

"This is delightful!" Jamal exclaimed. "It's like eating a big cinnamon roll. I've never had anything so rich and flavorful." He turned to Ronnie. "We must get down to the Beale Street soon. I've always wanted to go."

Victor raised his fork. "It's quite delectable, Sam. Please thank the chef for us."

Sam grinned. "I'm quite happy you like it."

Annoyance forgotten, Olivia hungrily devoured the cake.

Marla picked at hers, frowning. "Why did you do this, Sam? To pick on me? You know I can't have children. Why even bother going to the trouble to rub it in my face like this? It's just plain cruel."

"I'm not rubbing anything in, dear sister. I only want to help. I want to help all of you!"

Ronnie said, "The only thing you're helping me out with is fattening up my thighs."

Olivia giggled and continued to eat. Suddenly her fork struck something hard. She pulled it out and laid it on the plate.

"Olivia's got the baby!" Ronnie exclaimed. "You're next!"

"Ha!" she scoffed, grimacing at the plastic toy. "I'm single, twenty-two, and have no plans for kids anytime soon. Hard pass."

Jamal blurted, "Hey, I've got a baby, too!

Victor added, "As do I."

Frowning, Marla held up a small plastic baby of her own. "Is this a joke, Sam?"

Ronnie dropped his baby on the table. "I think the baker got a little over anxious."

Sam said, "No. No joke at all. Only life beginning anew."

Marla suddenly seized the table with both hands and went rigid. Her eyes bulged, her face shaking.

Victor stood and grabbed his wife. "Honey! What's wrong?"

Hissing out a long breath, Marla screamed and dropped back in her seat. Olivia stood with her brother and his boyfriend and rushed to Marla's side. Marla huffed and thrashed, and her husband screamed for someone to call 911. Then Victor began to scream. He collapsed to his knees, holding his stomach. Ronnie and Jamal both stared at one another before they, too, crumpled to the floor.

Olivia slowly backed away. She turned to her eldest sister, who smiled greedily at her siblings and their loved ones. She held an offering hand out to Olivia. "Yes, you, too."

Then she felt it—a massive swelling in her abdomen. At first it felt like indigestion, then it ballooned until her feet couldn't handle it. She dropped to the wooden floor, her screams joining her family's. She writhed uncontrollably, her teeth biting chunks out of her cheeks. The pain was excruciating, and it continued to worsen. She carefully rolled onto her back and pulled her blouse up over her pale stomach. Her belly stretched and expanded, like someone was inflating a basketball. She managed to glance over at her siblings and their partners. Marla cried and held her belly, while Victor and the other three men screamed and vomited. They held their hands over their distended stomachs, as if afraid to touch them.

From the living room, all five of Sam's girls quietly entered the dining area and stood by their mother's side. The oldest one asked, "Mommy, are we finally going to get some cousins to play with?"

Cain put an arm around his wife. Sam beamed, "By the grace of God, yes. Mother would be so proud of all of you."

Story Notes

We went to a party at my wife's best friend's house last summer. They had just gotten back from New Orleans for vacation, and they brought back a King Cake to serve to everyone. I had never even heard of a King Cake before that. If you haven't had one, much like it's explained in the story, they're really delicious and they're basically a giant cinnamon roll. And no, I didn't get the baby that night, no matter how much I wanted it. The story pretty much wrote itself.

NOW YOU DON'T

His cold wet nose pressed against the glass, Gunner waited with waning patience. A long, pitiful whine escaped his throat. It was the same thing every day, and the hours and minutes dragged by in an endless loop. He didn't want to sleep, eat, or even play with his new squeaky toy Mom brought home last week. He aimed to stay perched on the back of the couch, eyes darting back and forth behind a smudged window. He wanted Denny.

"Gunner! Get down from there right this instant!"

Gunner turned his head, ears flopping in his vision, as Mom came stomping into the living room. Gunner didn't like her. She yelled at him quite a bit, especially when he went potty inside the house. He hated being yelled at—most loud noises terrified him. Sometimes he yelled back, and when he did it felt good.

"I just cleaned those windows yesterday and now they're all smudged up again. I swear, you dachshunds are the most stubborn dogs alive." She crossed the room and put her hands under his stomach.

Gunner barked and bared his teeth.

"Denny will be home in a few minutes," she said, picking him up and placing him on the floor. "You can wait for him down here. Now go lay down."

Gunner, in fact, did not lay down. The moment her hands left his tiny body, he leapt back onto the couch and reclaimed his warmed spot at the window.

Mom sighed and walked back to her computer chair in the other room. "You never listen, do you? Fine. I forgot *you* pay the bills around here. Have it your way then, sire."

Eyes back out the window, he whined again, really letting it drag out this time.

After an eternity passed, a large yellow vehicle came into view at the end of the street. Gunner sat up straight-away. Heart racing, he barked and bounded off the couch the moment Denny stepped off the bus. Gunner raced to the hallway. Since he had no way of opening the door himself, he waited impatiently, his tail shaking hard enough to throw him off balance.

Dazzling sunlight filled the foyer as Denny stepped inside. Gunner was so happy, so over-the-moon, he couldn't help himself but to bark.

"Gunner!" Denny shouted. "Hey there, you little wienie!" He threw that big bulky thing off his back and dropped down to his knees.

Now more at eye level, Gunner pounced and stretched up to kiss him. Denny laughed and kissed him back. The boy's hands felt like pure heaven. It's all he ever wanted.

"Alright, Gunny, that's enough. Hey, boy. I've got something really fun to show you!"

Gunner's ears perked, but his mind was already on something else. He needed to go potty.

"Close that door right now, Dennis," Mom yelled from the other room. "You're letting all the cold air out."

"In a minute, Mom! I have to show you guys something!" He began to race up the stairs, but turned back to Gunner. "Stay here, boy. I'll be right back."

Gunner whined and started to hop up the stairs after him.

"No, Gunner! Stay down here. I'll be right back. Man, you never listen, do you?" The boy bounded up the steps without him.

A few prolonged moments later, Denny came back down with a long white sheet in his grip, and Gunner followed him back into the living room. With his foot he nudged Gunner to the middle of the room and told him to sit still. "Hey, Mom, come see what I learned at school today!"

"Hon, I'm busy working right now," she called from the other room. "Show me later, ok?"

"Please, Mom! I promise, it's really cool. Please?"

His mother huffed and stepped into the middle of the room with Gunner. Gunner took a few steps away from her. "Alright, but make it quick. I've got to get these reports turned in by four."

Grinning ear to ear, Denny backed himself up until he was directly under the doorway. "Brandon showed me this video today about how to do this. It's really neat, and it's going to freak Gunner out! Just watch."

Gunner perked up at his name.

"Alright, Gunny. Now stay right there and watch this." Gripping the sheet with both hands, the boy lifted it as high as his arms could reach. Other than his fingers, nothing of him was visible behind the white cotton blockade. "You ready, Mom? Gunny?"

Gunner barked.

"Yep," Mom said, arms crossed.

The sheet dropped, and behind it, the boy was gone.

Gunner took a few steps forward, but stopped. Heart hammering, he whined and barked twice. Where did Denny go?

Mom grinned, "Wow, hon, that was really neat!" She looked down to Gunner. "Where did he go?"

Panicked, Gunner bounded for the doorway, his little nails tapping the wooden floor, and searched both sides of the sunlit hallway. Nothing. He whined, then ran for the kitchen. He wasn't there, either. He didn't like this, not one bit. All he wanted was to play with Denny, maybe lie on the couch while the boy rubbed him until he fell asleep. This wasn't fun. Did Denny think this was fun? He hurried back into the living room, just in case Denny was hiding in there.

Over by the sliding back door, Mom studied the white sheet in her hands. "Hey, Gunner! Watch this!" Like Denny, she lifted the sheet high over her head, and like Denny she, too, was gone when it hit the floor.

Gunner didn't know what to do but bark. His cries echoed through the empty house, and there was nobody there to calm him. This wasn't fun! This wasn't what he wanted! He ran to the back door, but made sure to give the white sheet a wide berth. He gingerly walked around it, and made his way into the dining room. Mom and Denny weren't there, or in the kitchen for that matter. All worked up, Gunner ran from room to room, downstairs and up, searching and calling out for his family. They had to be there somewhere. They didn't say goodbye to him, didn't pat him on the head. He didn't see them leave the front—

The front door!

As fast as his little legs could carry him, Gunner hopped down the steps and darted out the wide-open front door. Maybe they were waiting outside for him! They'd laugh, and he would yell at them, and they would scoop him up and kiss him on the head. Only Denny could do that. He didn't like Mom as much.

The front yard was vacant, but as soon as his feet hit the front steps, a car pulled up in the driveway. Gunner barked happily when Dad stepped out of the vehicle.

"Hey, buddy!" Dad said happily. "How's my big guy doing today?"

Gunner barked back, twice.

Dad glanced back at the open door. "Where's Denzo and Mom, buddy? I've got something to show you guys."

Again, Gunner barked back. He looked at the house, then back to Dad.

"Eh, that's alright," he said. "I'll just show you." Dad leaned into the open car door and produced a clean white sheet from the front seat.

Gunner whined and took a few small steps back.

"It's alright, buddy. I promise this is really neat. Just watch." Dad stepped out into the open yard, lifted the sheet over his head, and dropped it.

Gone.

Gunner lost it. Confused and upset, he barked over and over, not sure what to do. He didn't want to go back into the house. Nobody was in there. He suddenly felt very small and alone, and that sad, empty feeling made him want to run and hide. So he ran. Through the front yard and out onto the sidewalk, he dashed down the road, searching for someone—anyone!—to help him find his family

Lucky for him, he found someone quickly. Three houses down, an old woman was sitting near her bushes, the ones where he sometimes went potty. Handfuls of weeds and grass littered the ground around her. Gunner made a beeline for her, barking to get her attention.

The old woman turned and appeared startled. She clutched her chest. "My word," she cried. "You frightened me something awful."

Gunner barked and barked. He backed up and turned toward his home, wanting the old woman to come with him. She helped him once before, when he left the back yard on his own, maybe she would help again.

"What's the matter, little one? You lost again?"

Gunner dropped down to his belly and barked.

"Poor little thing," the old woman cooed. She sat up on her knees, groaning. "Alright. Let's get you back home. I'm sure Denny boy is worried sick. That boy always said you never listen, getting yourself lost and all."

At the mention of Denny, Gunner quickly popped back up and turned around.

"But before we go, little one, I have to show you something."

Behind him the bush limbs rustled, and Gunner turned around just in time to see the old woman pulling a clean white sheet out from between them. Gunner growled and quickly backed away. On her knees, she lifted the sheet and let it fall. Gunner raced across the empty yard toward the street.

He knew the neighborhood well, had spent his entire life roaming the street, exploring every bush and hidey-hole. He played with the other two like him that lived at the opposite end of the block. He hated the weird thing across the street that hissed and chased him away. Sometimes he was given tasty treats by the people next door. But now, nothing seemed familiar. Everything felt wrong. Everyone was downright frightening.

Which was why he hesitated when three young boys drove up to him on their bikes. Gunner halted in his tracks and stayed low. He growled, a bark teetering at the tip of his tongue.

The three boys dropped their bikes. The biggest one said, "Hey, look! It's Denny's dumb little wiener dog!"

Another one laughed. "It looks like a dick with feet!"

The third boy stepped toward Gunner. "Where's Denny, you ugly little shit?"

Gunner didn't like the way the boy said Denny's name, and he definitely didn't like that the boy kept getting closer to him. Gunner continued to back up and growl.

"Where you going, mutt? Don't you run away from us!"

The closest boy dipped down and tried to grab him, but Gunner was faster. Gunner sidestepped and took off.

"Dumb dog doesn't listen, does he?" a boy yelled.

Gunner yelped as a rock dropped down in his running path. He leapt sideways, and another large rock pelted the street beside him.

"Get back here, dog! We just want to show you something!"

Then it got quiet. When Gunner realized the boys had stopped yelling, he skidded to a halt and spun around just in time to see a large white sheet falling listlessly to the ground. Catching his breath, Gunner slowly trotted back to where the boys had been.

Gunner barked at the white sheet as he approached. It didn't look strange or even smell any different than the ones Denny had on his bed. He stepped closer and closer, ready for it to jump at him and try to grab him like those boys. It remained lifeless, save for the wind ruffling its corners. Gunner touched it with his paw and jumped back. When it didn't attack back, he carefully nudged the sheet with his nose and he slowly pushed his head underneath.

"Gunner!" they cried.

He recoiled at their voices, but his heart fluttered with excitement. He looked down, and they were all there staring up at him, even people he had never seen before. Denny cried and reached up to grab him, but it was too high.

"Gunny!" the boy wept. "Help us!"

Dad scratched at the sides of the wall. "You have to help us, Gunner!"

Mom and the old woman yelled, "We need help, boy! Please, go get us help!"

Gunner wagged his tail and barked harder than he ever had before. He was so happy, so utterly ecstatic to see them again, even those boys that threw rocks at him.

Tears ran down Mom's reddened face. "For the love of God, Gunner, for once in your life just listen to us and go get help!"

"Find us help, Gunny!" Denny wept and buried his face in Dad's chest.

Gunner whined, not wanting to see Denny sad. It made him sad when Denny cried.

He knew just what to do!

Gunner backed up a few steps and wiggled his rear end.

Eyes wide, everyone below him shook their heads and threw their hands up. "NO!" they screamed.

He jumped.

Story Notes

There was an internet viral trend about a year ago where people were tricking their animals into thinking they disappeared behind sheets by running away and hiding before the sheet dropped. It was kind of cute at first, but after a while I started to feel bad for the animals. They don't know they were being played with. Most animals, especially dogs, think every time you step outside without them, you're never coming back. Whether you think it's funny or slightly cruel, it makes for an interesting story idea. Up to this point I had never written in the POV of an animal, so it was a bit of a unique experience.

LIP SERVICE

At 2:26 AM, Noel awoke with a startled yelp. His body went rigid. His heart leapt, and his teeth chattered.

Someone was sucking on his big toe.

He kept his eyes closed tight, terrified to move or make a noise. Someone had broken into his tiny apartment and was now violating him under the blanket where he slept. He listened hard for anything, any indication of who it might be. He had no girlfriend, so that was ruled out. The only other people living in his building were an old Mexican couple, Modesto and Glenda, who lived across the hall, and his landlord, a middle aged woman named Jeanette with bright red curly hair, who occupied the only upstairs loft, and she kept mostly to herself. He doubted any of them had a single reason to sneak into his home in the middle of the night to run their lips across the coarse skin of his hairy, big toe.

Many terrifying options ran through his head. In the pitch black of the room, for all he knew it could have been some crackhead or a crazed escaped convict—a giant bald murderer with hairy shoulders and no shirt pinning him down to the bed, ready to defile him, and he would be powerless to stop it. But he knew that wasn't the case. There was nobody holding him down.

In fact, he didn't feel anyone on the bed with him at all.

The sucking continued.

Mercifully, there was nothing menacing about it. The lips were almost loving in their slow, gentle strokes. The skin soft and moist around his rough flesh. No tongue or teeth to speak of. With motions so fluid he had no idea if they were male or female.

After a few minutes of letting it happen, he relaxed and willed himself to open his eyes. As expected, his bedroom was smothered in black, the only light coming from the clock on his nightstand. When his eyes adjusted, he lifted his head to focus on the foot of the bed and what was sucking on his foot.

Nothing.

Not a raise in the blanket, nor a single spot to zero in on.

Nothing.

Slowly, he laid his head back down and continued to let whoever—whatever—felate the big toe on his left foot. Before he knew it, he fell back to sleep.

***

Noel left for work the next morning more confused than he'd ever been. He wanted to chalk it up to some weird sex dream, from a mind who had not even seen a naked woman in months. The pink rash around his big toe told him otherwise. It didn't necessarily hurt, only itched a bit, but it should not have been there in the first place. He couldn't tell anyone. What would he say? Some creep with a foot fetish broke into his apartment at two in the morning to suck on his feet? Maybe they were going for his dick…or thought his big toe *was* his dick?

Fuck that noise.

Work went by quickly, as did his English Literature night classes at the college. When he got home later that night, he stopped before he opened his front door. He gingerly inspected both the top and bottom locks and found them to be unmolested (unlike his toe) and in good working shape. No wood splinters or jimmy marks in the doorframe. He stepped into his apartment and locked the door behind him.

He promptly went from room to room, checking every lock and window for signs of intrusion. Let's face it: he did this most nights anyway. Unfortunately, he lived in an unsavory part of town, in a ratty apartment building he never would have dreamed he would ever step foot in, but rent was cheap and parking was free. Water not included. His parents were never going to help with his living situation. Both were barely functioning alcoholics and could hardly afford to keep a roof over their own head, much less kick in on his student loans, so this is what he was stuck with. He made the best of it.

***

Once again, at 2:26 AM, he awoke to that same jarring feeling. He jerked awake to the sensation of lips on his big toe. Up and down they went, smooth and indubitably sensual.

Only this time there were two more pairs.

One was taking his pinkie toe on the same foot. The other sucking the middle toe on his right foot. The sensation was so inexplicably odd that it started to turn him on. He'd been so busy lately he hadn't even thought of masturbating, much less finding a woman to do something similar to what these disembodied lips were doing at that very moment. He wanted desperately to rip the blanket off his body to reveal what was doing this to him, but he feared what he might see. He feared he would scare them off.

To be perfectly honest, he was kind of enjoying it.

***

In the blink of an eye work was done, and before he knew it he was shutting down his computer and saying goodbye to his classmates as he jumped into his ancient Honda Civic and sped home from school. He couldn't wait to fall asleep. He couldn't wait to see what happened next.

But he wasn't tired quite yet.

As he paced the apartment, his mind raced. He didn't bother to wonder what the night suckers looked like, or even where they came from. They didn't even scare him anymore. If anything, they made him feel safe. Secure. He hadn't slept in the same bed with someone since high school, when his parents let his then girlfriend, Evonna, stay the night on the weekends. He hated the feeling of being alone: sleeping alone, waking up alone, eating alone, Netflix and Chilling alone. Life was mind-numbingly boring. He didn't spend much time fraternizing with co-workers, or even his peers at school—mostly "Hellos and goodbyes", "How are the kids?", "That eczema on your arm looks itchy."

The lips made him feel...wanted. Desired. A little less alone.

Restless, he threw himself on the couch and flipped through the digital TV guide and settled on a rerun of Modern Family. He watched as Sofia Vergara butchered the English language through her large, plump Spanish lips. He was fascinated. He flipped the channels until he came across some unnamable Angelina Jolie assassin flick. Angie's big, soft lips immediately grasped his attention. He leaned forward on the couch, enraptured. Once that was over, he found Liv Tyler on horseback being chased through the forest by men in black cloaks, while a sick midget clung to her for dear life. He spread his bare toes and absentmindedly itched them until they hurt. Slack jawed, Noel nearly drooled on himself as the she-elf, with a wide mouth just like her real life, rock star daddy's, told the midget he needed to stay awake and hold on. He shivered, then clicked the TV off and went straight to bed.

***

At nearly half past two the lips returned, bringing several more of their enthusiastic friends with them. Not only was every toe being taken care of, but both of his nipples now had guests.

They made no sounds. They used no tongues. They only sucked, up and down. Never slowing, ever gentile.

And always gone in the morning.

***

Noel opted to use a personal day instead of going to work, and he let his professors know he would not be in tonight, instead finishing his work from home on his laptop. He hated wasting what little vacation he had accrued, but he had no desire to spend his day stuffing legal envelopes for the Man, nor did he feel like letting his professor put him to sleep with another lecture on Friedrich Nietzsche's humdrum philosophies. Feet and chest throbbing and raw, he would rather spend the day at home. In bed. Hoping *they* would come.

But they never did.

On and off, he napped throughout the day, waiting patiently for his numerous little soft-skinned lovers to lull him into submission. But every time he woke it was of his own accord. By midday he was disappointed and tried to stay busy, but he didn't stray too far from the sofa or his bed. It hurt to walk, but he managed to shower and clean himself thoroughly with a brand new bottle of body wash.

The last thing he wanted was to taste bad.

***

They woke him once more at four minutes until 2:30 AM, after he passed out of sheer boredom. He was not waking up in fear as he once had, now his eyes opening slowly, dreamily, with a coy smile on his face.

They were all over him tonight. Now faster than before, they worked every free digit on his hands and feet. He spread his fingers and toes, allowing each separate pair of lips the freedom to move in their fervent ways. Both nipples were taken care of, and now two more had found their way up to his earlobes. He half expected to hear a heavy breathing in his ear, or hot wistful sighs on his cheeks, but the lips remained silent.

***

Work wasn't an option any longer. At this point Noel could barely walk without pain. His entire body was a hive of bright angry red rashes. He didn't need his coworkers to see him like this—not that he really cared what they thought of him anyway—but no sense in giving them a reason to talk. Within a week he used the rest of his vacation time, and two weeks in he had quickly run out of excuses for why he wasn't showing up to do his job. He quit. Fuck them.

His college professors, on the other hand, did not care if he showed up. They got paid either way.

In those few weeks, the only human interaction he had was with his ruby-headed landlord, to which they spoke a few words through a crack in the door and only about his late rent. He begrudgingly paid her with the last of his final paycheck then told her to piss off while slamming the door in her face. She didn't look too hurt by it.

**

His body throbbed from the sheer number of them that were now spread across his naked body. For weeks, more and more showed up on a nightly basis. When they ran out of outward extremities they attached to the wrinkly skin of his knee caps and elbows, then found his nose and nostrils. He was forced to breathe from his mouth. His breaths were sharp and hoarse, the pain plentiful. The newly sucked skin sang, but the old spots were numb and dead.

He did not panic. He'd grown to love his visitors and didn't want them to leave. So he let them be, allowing them to fill his nights with motion and appreciation.

***

When was the last time he had eaten? Had a bowel movement? Left the bed? He didn't think he was shitting himself or soiling the bed, but he couldn't be sure. His entire body trembled and quaked in unremitting pain. His head throbbed. What little skin he could still feel burned like fire. He was starving but didn't want to leave his bedroom—couldn't leave the bedroom. The pain in his feet had reached an unbearable state. When he could manage the strength to lift his head to look under the blankets, what he found was unsightly.

Most of his bare body was an angry mess of crimson welts and rashes. Tiny, blood-filled bumps littered his chest and arms like freckles, and what he could feel of his back was breaking out in bedsores. He dropped the blanket and wept. Never in his life had he been in such pain—never knew the toll it took on a person's mental capacity for tolerance. He didn't want to hurt anymore. He just wanted to sleep.

He just wanted *them*.

***

Like clockwork they came, quiet and consistent. Every inch of skin was now covered by the bodiless lips, sucking and grinding away at Noel's last ounces of sanity. More and more flocked to him, tiny and plump. Somehow he felt every pair meeting his skin.

Faster and faster. Feverous. Almost angry.

A loud moan escaped his mouth.

Then came their teeth.

A scream ripped through his throat as every individual mouth suddenly bit their desired area. Skin broke, and blood flowed freely into their mouths. Before he could really shriek, a large pair of lips covered his mouth, stifling his agony. With the ones already covering his nose, Noel lurched in the bed. He tried hard to thrash his arms and legs, but he was so weak they came as a little more than slight spasms. He was powerless.

There was nothing he could do. He let them feed.

Who was he to stop them?

***

From high above, everything seemed…familiar. Known. The room, though somewhat recognizable, appeared strange and unexpected. That's not where his dresser was supposed to be. The bed was at a weird angle, not by the window where he liked it, but now in the corner of the room, against the far wall. What was with that ugly painting by the door? And the wax warmer on the window sill? He'd never owned one of those.

The bathroom light snapped off, and a middle aged man—someone Noel had never seen before—stepped into the bedroom. Smiling, the man crossed his arms and nodded, looking happily around the room. Noel's room. The man then stripped nude, placing his clothes in a laundry basket, and turned off the bedroom light and jumped into bed. Before long he was snoring.

Noel watched all this impassively. He only focused on the clock on the nightstand.

He could not stop thinking about the man's big toe.

The digital numbers changed to 2:26 AM.

He was suddenly very hungry.

Story Notes

A few years ago, I decided I was going to start carrying a notebook with me to work. I was going to write down any idea that popped into my head, no matter how weird it was, just so I wouldn't forget it. I got to work that morning and the first thought I had was, "Wouldn't it be weird to wake up and find someone sucking on your toes?" I wrote it down, and over the next eight hours the whole story wrote itself in my head. This story has been a favorite of mine to take to readings, and the last time I read it to a crowd at Scares That Care Weekend in Williamsburg, VA I threw wax lips at the people listening every time I said the word 'lips.' It was a lot of fun.

BUST TO DUST

Tears rolling down his face, Jesse flicked the big red switch, and the machine roared to life.

"Dear Lord…why do you continue to take from me? Have I not been your faithful servant? Have I not done everything you have asked of me? Have I not given my life to you: my hours, my minutes? Have I not given you my blood, sweat and tears, blindly and without question?"

He leaned forward on the stool to grab the snarling black tube from the floor.

"I have given you everything—*everything!*—and all I have asked for in return is a child for my wife and I. A healthy child to call our own." Jesse dropped his head, thankful his cries would not be heard outside the walls of the small shed. "We lost another today, my Lord…although I'm sure you know that by now. I don't know what happened. We were so damn careful this time. We learned from our mistakes; we did everything right." He choked back a sob. "So much blood. Even more than last time. I don't think we can do it again. Her body and my mind just won't be able to handle it."

He sighed and adjusted himself in his seat. "I have nothing, Lord. Nothing left to give. Not even my dignity."

Without another word, he lifted the black tubing of the shop vac and placed its open barrel over his erection. Once the opening found his pubic mound and suction was fully optimized, the large vacuum canister whined in protest, making the tool shed seem that much smaller. Jesse moaned, his head dropping back, eyes closed.

It was his guilty pleasure, and no one—not even his beautiful wife, Valerie—knew of this. Nor would she ever. It would devastate her, end their marriage, and label him a sicko...but he couldn't stop. He'd been using the shop vac, the one they had received as a wedding present from her parents, for his masturbatory fun for several years. Anytime he felt the urge—and let's face it, the urge was strong and regular—he would sneak off to the yard barn in the backyard and relieve himself. It was a sickness, he knew, one that started as a teenager and never let up as an adult, but with a wife that wasn't nearly as sexually deviant as he, it made it difficult to stay satisfied. He needed this. No matter how terrible it made him feel right then.

Jesse moaned at the pressure building in his groin, trying to push away the image of his wife back inside the house, alone in their bed, crying at the loss of yet another would-be-addition to their family. He focused on his approaching climax—but only loss filled his mind's eye.

The ride to the hospital.

Red running down Val's thighs.

A silent shake of a doctor's head.

Quicker, he jerked the vacuum barrel up and down.

Then he cried, "I'm sorry, Val! I'm sorry I can't give you the family you want!" He gripped the seat of the chair with his free hand, his legs stiffening. "Lord, please! I'll do anything! I'll end these sins I commit in this shed! I'll stop treating this machine like a whore of Babylon! Please say something, and show me my pleas fall on caring ears!"

A deep, powerful voice reverberated through his skull. "*Anything?*"

"YES!" he screamed.

"*Then finish.*"

And with those words, he exploded, once again releasing his seed into the vacuum canister where hundreds of other loads of sperm resided. Jesse wept with pleasure; the orgasm brought fresh tears. His lord had finally spoken to him, renewing his faith once more. He dropped the vacuum barrel and clicked the machine off, his labored breaths cutting the silence.

He waited a few moments before asking, "What now, my Lord?"

The quiet was broken when the vacuum shook. Startled, Jesse nearly fell back off the stool.

Something stirred within the canister.

Without hesitation, Jesse unclipped its latches and threw the lid to the side. He dropped to his knees and triumphantly threw his hands skyward. "God is great!"

A gooey, dust-covered miracle cooed and reached out for its father.

Story Notes

I came across a webzine a few years back that was looking for "The craziest flash story you can send us." I didn't have anything at the time, but it came to me one night in bed when trying to go to sleep. I pitched the idea to my wife, and when I had her laughing, I knew I had something. I never heard back from that website, but I did find a religious horror anthology that happily accepted it. I still get a kick that I got paid for a story about a guy jerking off with a shop vac. Much like *He Loves Me Not*, this is another one my dad absolutely loves. He still brings it up pretty regularly and laughs about it.

RESISTING MADNESS

-1-

Gloria's agonized screams engulfed the tiny hospital room, and I couldn't have been a happier man. I'd been waiting for that day for most of my life. I know, I know, it's a weird thing for a guy to say he'd been dreaming of being a father since he was little, but there I was, heart swelling with pride and pockets full of bubblegum cigars.

My little boy was almost here.

Over the course of thirty-six hours—yes, you heard me right, thirty-six miserable, sleepless fucking hours—I had gripped my wife's hand like my whole world depended on it. I helped her to concentrate on her breathing, massaged her back with a tennis ball as instructed in the Lamaze classes, and got her anything the doctors allowed me to bring to help her. I would have done anything to ease Gloria's pain. I would have killed for her.

Nearly two days of not showering had plastered most of her long blond hair against her head, and the rest had clumped up and was stuck to her sweat-stained pillow. Combined with my own ripe odors, the glossy white delivery room was a cloud of stink so thick you could slice it like warm sourdough.

I recall being so damn hungry it made me sick. I sometimes went days without eating while I was on set—depending on how busy I was prepping scenes or applying prosthetics—but the older I got, the more I couldn't handle going that long between meals. But if my wife was only allowed ice chips during labor, then I would suffer with her. It was the very least I could do.

I remember the way she looked that day. Even though she was a mess, she was still so beautiful, everything I grew up wanting in a woman. As cliché as it sounded, I didn't deserve her. She was an aspiring actress, well on her way to the top of Hollywood. I was slumming it in the back room, creating makeup effects and monsters like my heroes before me. She could have been with anyone—any pretty smile or tight ass with a bigger paycheck. But she chose me. This schlub.

That fucking bitch.

Regardless of how I feel now, back then I loved her like crazy. We grew in Hollywood together. The further she ascended to stardom, the higher I rose in the special effects world. Since my teens, I had aimed to be the next Tom Savini, and I'd be damned if I wasn't going to surpass his illustrious career by the time I was in my thirties. With Gloria by my side, I could have done anything. And we did.

The nurse handed me another damp rag, which I used to pat Gloria's forehead. "Keep breathing, baby, you've got this. He's almost here."

Teeth gritted, Gloria grunted, "I *am* breathing, dickhead! I've been breathing my whole life! I know how to breathe!"

I grimaced. "I know, I know. I'm just trying to help."

"You want to help? Have this baby for me!"

"Baby, believe me, if I could, I would gladly *Junior* the shit out of this for you. Unfortunately, I don't have childbearing hips."

Through the pain, she muttered a laugh. "That movie sucked."

"Yeah, it's no *Kindergarten Cop*."

"Martin," Doctor Minor interjected, peering up between my wife's legs, "would you like to talk Schwarzenegger films or would you like to help Gloria to push?"

"Sorry, doc."

"It's quite alright," he said, dipping back down between the stirrups. "And for your information, *Twins* is a much better film than both of those."

I chuckled. "In what world—"

"Gloria, I need you to push," the doctor snapped. "He's crowning now. It looks like he's ready to finally come out."

Quickly I knelt down and got close to my wife's face. "You hear that, baby? Just a few more big pushes. I'm right here with you."

"You can be right here for me about a foot further back," she groaned. "Your breath smells like shit."

"Sorry," I said, standing back up.

Doctor Minor eyed me. "Would you like to come down here and watch your son meet the world, daddy?"

I thought about it, then shook my head. "No, I think I'm good. I'd rather remember what that looked like down there before she gives birth."

The doctor snickered, and Gloria blurted out a long painful scream.

Doctor Minor regained his composure. "Alright, Gloria, I need you to take in a deep breath through your nose, and as you exhale, give me one good push. Can you do that for me?"

Gloria nodded vigorously.

"Ok. Deep breath…and push!"

It seemed like hours after that. I kept my hand firmly in hers, even though her grip brought tears to my eyes. I didn't need the help. I was already crying. In those long moments I was running the future in my mind's eye.

Passing on my loves and passions to my son, in hopes he would follow in my footsteps. Watching movies with him. Taking him to Dodgers games. Eating the biggest pizza we could find. My wife may have been my best friend, but at the moment, she was giving birth to my best buddy.

All eight pounds and five ounces of Nolan Michael Wiger was born at five fifty-two PM on January eighteenth.

Nothing was ever the same after that.

I didn't see him at first. I only heard his cries and the quick snip of the umbilical cord. Tears streamed down my cheeks, and I buried my lips into my wife's. "You did it, babe."

Still catching her breath, she nodded and added her tears to mine.

Nolan continued to wail as the nurse swaddled him in a blue blanket.

"He's got your lungs," I laughed.

"That's your whining I hear," she added.

Doctor Minor stood up and took off his gloves. "Congratulations, you two."

"Would you like to hold him?" the nurse asked us.

"Yes," Gloria croaked with a dry throat.

My newborn in her arms, the nurse walked over to my side of the bed. "He's so prec—" She stopped walking. Her eyes were locked onto my child's.

I still couldn't see my son, but her wide, horrified eyes told me something was wrong. "Nurse?"

She didn't move, didn't speak. Her eyes remained as wide as they could possibly stretch. Her lips gradually opened in a tight O, then pulled back over her teeth like a cornered animal. The nurse's chest hitched in and out, and her arms trembled under my child's diminutive weight.

I stood and stepped toward the nurse. "Nurse? What's wrong?"

Then she screamed.

I've spent most of my life on movie sets. Being in the horror business, I had heard all manner of screams from actresses, ranging from casting call amateurs all the way up to the women who were paid the big bucks to find the terror deep down in their guts. I was numb to it by that point, had heard it every which way til Sunday. But this was different. This was real. This was pure, soul-crushing pain.

Doctor Minor scrambled to her. "My God, Nurse Savory! What in the hell are you doing?"

Gloria yelled, "What's wrong with my baby?"

The doctor, now standing next to her, had gone silent. His head was down, staring at my swaddled child, who wailed right along with the nurse.

I stepped up between them, desperate to take my son in my arms. "Give me my child. Right now!"

I almost couldn't hear what the doctor said, but between screams he whispered, "Those eyes…" Then he, too, added to the noise.

Gloria tried to sit up in bed, but she was too weak. She fell backwards, crying. "What's wrong with my baby? Give me my baby!"

Heart pounding, I wedged myself between the two and reached for my child.

Two things happened very quickly. The nurse threw her arms up and clutched at her ears. The doctor grabbed me by the shoulders and screamed directly into my face.

In a blind panic, I twisted from his grip and dove to the floor. I thought for sure I would miss Nolan and my child would thump on the floor in front of me, but thankfully, the only thump was made by me as I dropped to my side, arms out. Nolan fell into my waiting hands. His frightened cries were pure pain to my ears. My instincts took over. I pulled his tiny, pinkish body close, his head buried in my chest, and scrambled backwards across the floor to the bed. Above me, Gloria bawled as she was too drained to raise up.

A few feet away, Doctor Minor and Nurse Savory continued to scream and thrash about the room. The nurse grabbed the instrument tray and, flinging the contents across the room, began to bash her head with the stainless steel plate. On his knees, the doctor pulled at the wreath of gray hair around his balding head, tearing out bloody chunks by the handful. Still screaming, he crawled toward the large vaginal speculum on the floor and shoved the stainless steel tool into his mouth. When the instrument wouldn't go in any further, he squeezed the trigger and the two sides widened. From across the room I heard his jaw muscles crack. Blood dribbled from the doctor's lips, followed by a torrent of red-tinged vomit, which pushed the instrument from his mouth to land with a clang among the gore.

I felt helpless, unable to comfort my terrified wife or the child I held tight against my chest. Nolan wailed and wiggled against me, and it took everything in my power not to look at his face. The chaos before me instructed me otherwise.

The nurse grunted and tossed the steel plate aside, then swiped a scalpel from the floor. She turned toward me, still screaming her lungs out, and drove the knife directly into her right eye. I yelled and pushed myself backwards until I could go no further. I pulled my knees up to my chest, mindful of Nolan, just as the nurse fell face-first to the linoleum floor. The scalpel made a wet swicking sound as it drove into her brain.

In his own agony, Doctor Minor stood up and ran for the wall. Over and over he bashed his head into the bank of hydrogen nozzles. Soon, he sank to his knees, and after one more head-butt, he fell over to his side. His final screams dissolved into wet gurgles that oozed onto the floor.

Now the only one left screaming was my wife. Her hands frantically reached for my head, pulling at my hair and my shirt collar. I sat there, shaking. I didn't dare let go of my son.

I refused to look into his newborn eyes.

-2-

Martin Wiger clicked the record button on his phone and sat back with a sigh. Over a decade of silence and every damn, disgusting detail was pouring out of him like a popped balloon. It wasn't hard to remember; it's not as if he was repressing the memory and only now, with intermittent nips of alcohol, was it trickling back. He saw it replay on the backs of his eyelids every night, and even on the blackest of ceilings when closing his eyes wouldn't erase the sights. No amount of chemicals would ever rid him of that day.

With a shaking hand, he placed his phone down on the desk among the various contracts and hand-scribbled notes, and replaced it with a glass of Wild Turkey. He preferred it on the rocks, but neat would have to do. He took a sip, then another, then drained the glass with a loud gulp. He hoped it would take the edge off, steady his hand, and wipe out the nerves that moshed around in his stomach. Nearly thirty years in the movie business and day one on set still made him feel like an anxious newbie.

This wasn't just another movie. Not this time.

A quick knock on the door behind him, and Andrew Macleod, Martin's longtime assistant director, poked his head into the dark room. "Hey, Marty. It's time."

Martin quickly shoved the empty glass and half-finished bottle into the bottom desk drawer and spun around. "Almost ready, Andy. Just give me a minute."

Eyebrow cocked, Andrew stepped into the room and clicked on the overhead light. Martin winced at the fluorescent attack. "Come on, damn it!"

The AD closed the door behind him. "Christ, Martin. You look like…"

"What? What do I look like, Andy?"

"Like shit. A whole bag of it."

"You've really got a way with words. Do you know that?"

Andrew stepped closer. "Well, what do you want me to say, man? That you look Tide clean? You look and smell like a Skid Row bum. How much have you had to drink today?"

Martin pointed. "I haven't had anything to drink today, for your information. I'm stone cold sober."

Hands on his hips, Andrew croaked out a laugh. "If you're stone cold sober, then I'm Stone Cold Steve Austin. Level with me, Marty. What's the matter?"

Andrew was a good kid, and one of his few crew members he regularly worked with that was able to speak to him the way he did. Martin didn't exactly lord over his production crews, but he expected respect. Decades of awards and accolades didn't just fall into his lap because he had wished them there. Andrew Macleod had been Martin's right-hand man for over a decade, and even though he was a bearded thirty-three-year-old and not some twenty-year-old, wide-eyed wannabe anymore, he still liked to think of him as a kid. There were numerous crew members he regularly employed—including his personal make-up effects crew, hand-picked and reared by him—Andrew was someone he could always count on to not be his *yes man*.

Martin rubbed his eyes. "I'm nervous."

"*Nervous?* What do you have to be *nervous* about? You're the great Martin Wiger! Horror make-up effects guru and director extraordinaire! Why, I once heard you moved a mountain just by thinking it!"

Martin shot him the bird. "Who am I? Bill Brasky?"

"Come on, Martin. What do have to be nervous about? You've done this hundreds of times."

"Christ, how old do you think I am?"

Andrew shrugged. "Old enough your balls dip in the toilet water when you sit down to shit."

Martin smiled at his friend and sighed. "I just can't believe this is it, Andy."

"Is that why you're nervous? For Christ's sake." He shook his head, perplexed. "This series is about to go out with a bang! *The Eyes of Madness part five*, man."

"The last one."

"The last one, my ass. We all know horror series never actually end. Look at Freddy and Jason? *Saw*? Hell, we're on, what, the second retconning of the *Halloween* series—where Jamie Lee Curtis conveniently forgets she was in, like, three sequels before this last one? We're going to milk your titty for all it's worth."

Martin stood from his chair. "Not this time, buddy. *This is it.*"

"What do you mean?"

"You'll see," Martin said, squeezing the shorter man's shoulder. "How do I look?"

Andrew examined him. "You could at least tuck your shirt in. And comb your hair. All the suits are out there with the cast and crew, waiting for you. The least you can do is look like you haven't been sleeping under an overpass."

He slumped with an exaggerated groan. "The suits…"

After adjusting himself in the mirror and a deep, enervated sigh, Martin stepped out onto the soundstage, Andrew closing the door behind him. Near the middle of the warehouse floor, between three different fully dressed sets, the cast and crew of nearly one hundred turned to look at him as one. Save for a few new faces, he recognized every single person. Over the years, whether through good fortune or the extent of his kindness, he had amassed an ever-reliable crew who followed him from project to project. Even when he wasn't directing, he helped place individuals in other jobs, as his recommendation was as good as gold. His star in Hollywood may have dimmed over the years, but his place in the annals of horror cinema certainly would not.

The gathering clapped heartily as he approached. A few even whistled.

This is going to be so fucking difficult.

Martin smiled and put his hand up for silence. After another thirty seconds passed, the applause died down.

"Christ almighty, everyone! I'm not here to accept an award."

A gentle laughter rolled through the crowd, punctuated by someone yelling, "You're the man, Marty!"

Martin turned to the voice. "No, you're *the man*. All of you are *the man*. Listen, I know it's day one of this shoot, and I know the last thing you all want to hear from me is some sentimental bullshit about how I love you and respect the hell out of you guys. We usually save this kind of sappy shit for the final cut of the shoot right before we all get blasted, but I've got some things I have to say before the camera rolls. I do love and respect you all. I have handpicked each and every one of you to be a part of this project, right down to the craft service people who make those killer cheesesteaks I like. I created this series fifteen years ago, and even though I've worked on numerous, more profitable projects over the years, this series will always be my baby. It may not seem like it, but these films have always been…personal…to me."

He paused. Swallowed.

"Maybe we should have stopped after the first one. Maybe we should have ended the series after part three. Let's be honest, the hidden daughter with mind control subplot from that one, well, that was my bad. But we pushed through." The few remaining crew members from that film chuckled, except for the three men in dark suits standing near the back.

The producers, including Floyd Golden, continued to listen to Martin's every word as if they were going to be his last. Martin gave them little more than a cursory glance.

"Anyway, so here we are, at *Part Five*," he continued. "The final film…my final film." All at once the voices around him rose, which he shushed by throwing his hands up. "Settle down, everyone. Settle down. I'm not dying. I'm just retiring. I've been in this business since I was a pup. I've done everything I could possibly do to drop my change in the horror bucket, but this is it for me." Martin struggled to hold back his emotions.

He glanced out at all of the faces frowning back at him. Patty Oswalt, from hair and make-up. Tommy Langan, the key grip. Eddie Meyer and Tito Vasquez, from the lighting department. Mickey Highmark, his longtime leading villain. Ted, Marlo, Lisa and Mike, the kids he taught everything about make-up effects to. He couldn't imagine not being around these people.

"This has been a long time coming for me. And I want this to be my last hurrah. I want to go out on top. I want *Part Five* to be the fucking horror film of the decade. Will you guys and gals go on this journey with me? Will you help me blow the rest of Hollywood out of the water and show them we can *actually* make a movie scarier than *The goddamn Exorcist?*"

A rowdy cheer erupted from the cast and crew. Martin, unable to hold back the tears, clapped along. Andrew threw an arm over his shoulder and, though he looked upset, congratulated him with a kiss on the cheek.

The producers continued to watch with indifference.

Martin grinned. "Now get to work, assholes!"

When the cast and crew scattered, Martin walked back to his office, suggesting with a nod that Andrew follow him.

"You son of a bitch," Andrew said. "Why didn't you tell me before everyone else?"

Martin pulled two cold Corona's from a hidden cooler by his desk and handed one to his AD. "Just shut up and drink, you whiner."

Andrew sipped his cold drink. "So what's next for the great Martin Wiger? Retirement…just doesn't seem like you."

Martin gulped down his beer without a word.

"I guess you could spend more time with Nolan. Right?"

A shiver dripped down Martin's spine. "That's the plan."

-3-

In a perfect world, with the southern California sun blessing all it touched, Martin would have been coaching a little league team to the state championship. He would have been riding bikes down the Venice boardwalk with his son, where the ice cream was so sweet it hurt your teeth. He would have been making love to Gloria under the orange trees in their back yard, with the Hollywood hills as their audience.

But this isn't a perfect world.

In perfect worlds, children aren't locked up in state hospitals for the criminally insane.

Norwalk, California was a short drive down I-5 from Martin's rundown apartment on the edge of Chinatown. At the height of his career, he had owned a beautiful four-bedroom ranch in Universal City, complete with a full FX studio in the basement where much of his early work had been created, and a sprawling yard with an in-ground pool and manzanita bushes he paid someone else to trim. But that was over five years and two incomes ago, and with little money coming in these days, he didn't have much of a choice where he lay his head. He wasn't broke, but there was a good reason he talked the studio into letting him write, direct, produce and run the special effects team on this movie, and it certainly wasn't because he was a workaholic.

The drive down to the hospital always gave him some much-needed quiet time. Time to think. Dwell. It took a lot to make him smile these days, but the few hours every other week he got to spend with Nolan were enough to make him happy. He was all Nolan had left in this world. Both of Martin's parents had long since passed, and Gloria left them both only a few years after the boy's birth. Martin had fought hard for her to stay. There was no diagnosis, no hard factual way of telling how or why their child was born with his terrible en-dowment, but she couldn't see past it or his love for the boy. The last he'd heard, she'd quit mainstream acting and had moved to the Valley, where she now took her clothes off and put things in her mouth for money. He didn't miss her one bit.

His musings were cut short the moment he pulled into the hospital's parking lot. Multiple ambulances and police cars were littered about the entrance, and there were more officers inside the building, blocking his way. Once he explained his reason for being there, he was allowed to pass and quickly made his way up to the juvenile ward on the fourth floor.

When the elevator doors whisked open, a nurse was sobbing uncontrollably against the opposite wall. Martin did his best not to stare. He turned down the long, brightly lit hallway and stopped. Though Nolan's room was the first door on his right, his attention was drawn to the walls. Every few feet, intermittent splotches of blood had blossomed on the cream-colored wallpaper. They appeared to zig-zag down the hallway, switching sides every few feet, until they disappeared out the large plate glass window at the end. Several police officers milled about the shattered window. The nurse behind him continued to cry.

Heart hammering, Martin burst into Nolan's room. He found two more officers cornering his now ten-year-old son in the back corner, while the Psychiatry Chief of Staff watched on in annoyance.

"What the fuck is going on in here?" Martin yelled as he shouldered past the officers.

"It's alright," Dr. Brolan told them. "That's his father."

Martin knelt down and stared at his boy's face. Behind the thick black goggles strapped across his eyes, was a terrified child barely into his double digits of life. His ear-length blonde hair was a disheveled mess, and his cheeks were puffy and flushed candy apple red. Nolan wept and threw his arms around his father's neck.

Martin growled, "What happened? What did you do to him?"

One of the officers, a tall white man with his head shaved in a crewcut, pointed at Nolan. "What did *we* do? Why don't you ask what this *little shit* did?"

Martin couldn't stand up quick enough. "The fuck did you just say?"

The other officer, a young Hispanic man, put his hand on Martin's chest. "Calm down, sir. We're trying to figure out what exactly happened here ourselves."

"Get your hand off me, damn it! I'm not going to stand here and listen to you insult my child. I've got lawyers that'll listen to that for me."

"Sir, just—"

"Why don't you stop telling me to calm down and try telling me what happened?"

The younger officer eyed the boy. "There's been an incident. About an hour ago. One of the nurses threw herself out the window after she was in the room with the patient."

"Nolan," Martin said. "The patient's *name* is Nolan."

The officer sighed. "Yes, Nolan. We were trying to question young Nolan here about what happened."

Martin turned toward the doctor. "And you didn't think to call me first?"

Dr. Brolan added his own sigh. "I was in the process of contacting you when these two *fine* officers insisted on speaking with your son. Listen, why don't Mr. Wiger and I go speak in private for a bit, then the four of us can speak together with a bit less hostility. Cooler heads, yes?"

Martin gritted his teeth. "Fine."

"Very good. Let's go to my office. Nolan can stay here. You two, if you wouldn't mind, please step out into the hallway. We'll only be a bit."

"Yeah, you and Officer Dickface can step the fuck out."

The bigger officer sneered, "Watch it, pal," and exited the room.

Kneeling back down to Nolan, Martin touched the boy's cheek. "Hey, bud, stop your crying, ok? Remember what I said before? If you cry with your goggles on, your eyeballs will drown."

That same old joke still made Nolan smile.

Before joining his partner, the young Hispanic officer asked, "By the way, Mr. Wiger, I'm a really big fan of your work. When you've got a second, could I have your autograph?"

***

Dr. Brolan's office was stuffy, crowded with old leather medical books, and felt every bit the part-time home of someone who lorded over the misfortunate and dependent. Martin had never liked Dr. Gordon Brolan, and if their bi-weekly encounters were any indication, the feeling was mutual. The man was cold and blunt, someone who had spent far too many years diagnosing and looking away. He was obviously very good at his job, and Martin knew it frustrated the doctor to no end that he had zero clue as to what affected Nolan.

Martin sat in the worn leather chair opposite of him. "So are you going to tell me what the hell's going on, or am I going to have to guess?"

Dr. Brolan folded his hands on his desk. "As you can see, we've had an unfortunate incident involving one of our nurses and your son, Mr. Wiger. At approximately eight forty-five this morning, one of our newest residents, Nurse Dries, entered your son's room to rouse him from his sleep. At some point in the night his goggles had loosened, and when Nurse Dries—who, mind you, has never worked hand-in-hand with young Nolan—went to readjust them, they came loose and fell off." He shook his head, like a bad taste had suddenly invaded his mouth. "When she became...*infected* with madness, she ran screaming out of the room and proceeded to bash her skull into the walls, from one side of the hallway to the other, until she ended her life by exiting through the picture window."

Martin could only grimace. "She should have known. They all should have known by now. Isn't it your job to teach them to never remove his goggles? I made those specifically so no one could see through them."

"She was new, just transferred here from Portland. She hadn't had time to be fully prepped for your child's…"

"What? My child's what?"

"*Ailment*," he spat. "His ailment."

Martin shrugged. "Look, I'm sorry for your nurse's death. It's tragic, but it never should have happened. I'm not taking responsibly for this, and neither will Nolan. You were given specific instructions. It's not my problem you couldn't follow them."

"I know it's not your fault," he snapped. "It's not even young Nolan's fault. Despite what you might think, I quite like your child. He's a sweet boy, always polite and respectful to myself and my staff. I only want what's best for the boy."

"As do I," Martin added.

"Which is why I'm moving him out of this facility."

Martin sat up straight. "Come again?"

"I cannot afford to watch over your child any longer, nor can I devote any more time to studying his condition. I've spent the last three years exhausting myself and my resources and, to be perfectly frank, Mr. Wiger…I'm at a complete loss."

"Well, no sh—"

"No, no," Dr. Brolan stopped him. "I'm talk-ing—you listen. When Nolan was brought to me three years ago, I made it my top priority to narrow down the cause of what makes your child unique. Never in my thirty-three years of practicing medicine have I ever come across a person who, for lack of a better way of phrasing it—because it frankly doesn't have an actual name—has what I refer to in my notes as The Devil's Eyes. I'm sure you're more than aware your son's eyes cause anyone who looks directly into them to go into a psychotic fit, which ends with them harming themselves, grievously. Most specifically to their heads. Mr. Wiger, I'm fresh out of politically correct terms. Your child's eyes cause absolute madness."

Martin knew all of this, but it made his stomach sink all the same. "Don't you think I know that, Doc? You weren't there the day he was born. You weren't there all the times he…"

"Are you aware he's caused the deaths of two oth-ers?"

Martin stared at him. "What?"

The older man nodded. "The night he was brought here, another patient, a young man with paranoid schizo-phrenia—who *should* have been in his room, mind you—was wandering the halls and somehow slipped into your son's room. We found him the next day in your son's bathroom with his skull bashed open, by his own accord, with the tank lid of the toilet. A year and a half ago one of our custodians bumped into Nolan in the hallway and knocked his goggles off. After ten minutes of breaking the door down, we found him in the storage closet with the handle of his broom shoved into his eye socket as far as it could go."

Despite the heat outside, Martin shivered. "Why am I just finding out about this?"

"Because it's not the sort of thing we like to publicize, Mr. Wiger. The patient had no living relatives, and the custodian was a widower with no children. Plus, we have very good lawyers, so no fretting about whether you'll be responsible for those two casualties. Or the one which occurred today. We may have wiped away those other two deaths, as we will with today's, but I can't have this happen again. Not here."

"Then where?"

"On July sixteenth, Nolan will be transferred to our sister facility in Lakewood, Washington—"

Martin's voice rose with a sharp edge. "*Washington?*"

"—where he will be kept in a much more structured environment, with more security."

"You can't do that!"

Dr. Brolan shook his head. "I'm afraid you're wrong, Mr. Wiger. I can, and I will. You lost your rights to Nolan three years ago when the state brought him into my care. You're lucky the courts even let you visit him as often as you do. Your son, despite his extreme shortcoming, is a sweet child, but I cannot have him in my facility any longer."

Standing quickly, Martin leaned over the desk into the doctor's face. "I'll fight this."

"That's your prerogative, Mr. Wiger. Do as you please, but I will not put my patients or my staff in harm's way any longer. I simply cannot stomach another unpleasant death under my roof." He glanced at the clock. "You've got another hour before your time is up for the day. I suggest you go spend it with your child while you can."

-4-

"And…action!"

With her teased-up fiery ginger hair, Vanessa took two hurried steps forward and yelled, "Harmond! I just saw him! He's outside, breaking through the gate!"

"Cut!"

Martin's leading man Corey Graves, a young African American actor who broke into Hollywood by way of

The Eyes of Madness Part Three, dropped his head and sighed. "What now, Marty?"

Sighing himself, Martin stomped around the camera toward his leading actress. "Vanessa, hon, how many times do I have to tell you to hit your mark? It's three steps—not two! It's a locked-down shot over Corey's shoulder! I can't shoot the scene when you're out of the damn shot!"

Corey crossed his arms. "How many more times do we have to do this scene, Van? There's literally a green X on the floor where you stop."

Frustrated, Vanessa threw her arms up and growled, "I'm trying! What do you want me do, Martin? I'm trying my best!"

"I want you to fucking act! That's what I want you to do. To speak the fucking lines and hit your fucking mark! Christ in Heaven, Noah over there is six-years-old and has no problem finding the big green X at his feet."

Across the room, the child actor was fast asleep on a couch, with a half-eaten Fruit Roll-Ups hanging off his cheek.

Though much shorter than Martin, Vanessa stepped up to him and jabbed a well-manicured nail into his chest. "How dare you! You don't speak to me that way! Who do you think you are?"

"I'm the asshole who gave you job, missy. So I suggest you get back to your mark, or you can go back to shooting Target ads for Tide Pod-eating Midwesterners in Indiana."

Vanessa stomped her feet. "Screw this! We've been shooting since five-thirty this morning. I'm done! I'm going to bed!" With that she trudged off the set, leaving behind the echo of her exasperations.

The day hadn't exactly been going according to plan. It was true, they had been up since before five thirty, but Martin, being the head of the production, was up even earlier. In fact, he hadn't slept in nearly two days. His eyes burned, and his hands shook, and his body odor was offensive, even to him. Nothing—absolutely *nothing*—was going right.

A little over two weeks into production, and they were already nearly three days behind schedule. He wanted to blame the actors, they were the easiest and most drama-filled excuses he could throw out. He could have very easily blamed the designers for half-assing the soundstage sets, when they very clearly should have been completed with their work months before the shoot. Even the very capable underlings in his effects department, the ones he spent years rearing into relevance, continued to drop the ball on an almost daily basis without his constant micromanagement. But in all truth, he could only blame himself for this mess.

Martin had spent years working himself to the top of his game. He had brought some of the fiercest and most outrageous monsters to the silver screen. He had directed some of the biggest genre films of the last two decades. He had discovered numerous other talented filmmakers and visionaries and helped them bring their ideas to life with his various companies and resources. Above all else, he liked to think he brought joy to all of his fans across the globe and made their lives a little more enjoyable. But amongst the several dozen crew members staring in his direction, not a single one of them appeared joyful. He was losing them, quickly, and for the first time in his career he had no idea how to right the ship.

Everything is falling apart.

Corey broke the silence. "Hey, man, are we, like, done for the night? I'm barely able to keep my eyes open."

Martin shook his head, confused. "What? No. We have to get this scene completed! This should have been finished hours ago!"

A warm hand on his shoulder made him flinch. Andrew, his Assistant Director, said, "Hey, Martin, man, let's just call it a night. What do you say? I really doubt Vanessa is coming back out of her trailer willingly."

"No, damn it! We've got to finish this. And why do you keep saying you're tired? It's not even late!"

Andrew frowned. "Marty…it's two-forty-five in the morning. The call sheet says we're supposed to be up in five hours to start shooting again."

A wave of dizziness washed over Martin. *Two-forty-five?* He took a deep breath, overly aware of the blood-shot eyes awaiting his response. "Yeah, ok. That's a wrap, everyone. We'll try again in a few hours. Good work. Get some sleep."

After a chorus of groans, the room quickly emptied out. Andrew leaned against the wall of the living room set and watched as Martin withdrew a flask from his pocket. "You can't do that, man."

"Eat a dick," Martin groaned after a heavy gulp. "I'm in charge, not you."

Andrew chuckled humorlessly. "Barely, my man. Barely." After a few moments he asked, "What's going on, Marty? I've never seen you this bad."

Martin sat on the couch with a sigh. His knees popped like gun blasts. "Well…I'm old, I've got Irritable Bowel Syndrome, and I can't eat fried chicken anymore because of it. How's that for a start?"

"Come on, man. Don't pull shit or bullshit with me."

Martin's mouth dried up as if it was full of cotton balls. "They're moving Nolan up to Washington state, to a fully secured hospital, where I won't get to see him. They can't handle him anymore. They've all but given up on him. Said he's hurt too many people there to justify him staying."

"Christ, man. I'm so sorry. What about you?"

"I haven't gotten official word, but I'm pretty sure I'm losing all my rights. I'm losing my son, Andy, and I don't know what to do." Hot tears embarrassed him as they dripped down his cheeks.

Andrew shook his head. "I don't know what to say, Marty. That's fucking terrible. You couldn't move up there?"

Martin snorted, "I can't even afford the roach motel I live in now. I'm nearly broke as it is. Have been since Gloria left. Why do you think I'm taking on everything with this movie? I meant to use this money to fight the courts and try to get Nolan out of there."

"I hate to ask this, Marty, because you know I love you like the big brother I never asked for, but why don't you step down for a while? Maybe let someone else take over the production while you get things straightened out?"

Martin took another nip from his flask. "No can do."

"Why? We've got other people who can steer the ship while you're gone, man. Family's more important than this shit."

Frowning, Martin said, "Are you trying to take my job, Andy?"

Andrew pulled a face. "*What?* No! For Christ's sake, that's not what I'm saying here, man. I'm just saying, regardless of what's happening with Nolan, it's becoming increasingly obvious you're overwhelming yourself with this project."

"Excuse me? What's that supposed to mean?"

Andrew, though much shorter, stepped up to Martin. "I'm saying I'm not the only one who's noticed you're slipping up. You're not sleeping, not showering. You're drinking on set."

"I'm not drinking on set!"

"What's that in your fucking hand?"

Martin, not realizing he'd been drinking at all, stared at the pewter container in his shaking hand. He closed the cap on the flask and then dropped it onto the couch.

"We're literally three days behind schedule, Marty," Andrew continued to spew. "You think the studio hasn't noticed? They've noticed alright. More and more of the producers have been milling about set, wondering what the fuck is wrong with the great Martin Wiger, and where is all their precious money going? They're asking questions, Marty, and I'm tired of giving them excuses."

Sadly, even with a brain half-dipped in spirits, Martin had noticed more suits on set than normal. He did his best to blow them off when he could, especially the ones who overstepped their boundaries like Floyd Golden and wanted to look through the lens themselves. Never in his decades of work in the film industry did he care to work side-by-side with his producers, much less memorize their names. They were faceless pocketbooks. They did their job, he did his.

"I'm sorry, Andy."

"I don't want your apologies, Marty! I want you to get your fucking act together. You're not the only one working on this movie. You've got a whole lot of cast and crew who are, much like you, depending on this paycheck. I can't afford to lose my job because you're going off the deep end. I'm real sorry about what's going on with Nolan. He's a real sweet kid and he doesn't deserve this, but neither do we."

A cool breeze swept through the stage as the AC clicked on. Martin shivered. He eyed the flask. "I'll try my best."

Andrew growled, "Well, your best needs to get a hell of a lot better," then stormed off.

As soon as he heard the back door slam shut, Martin swiped the flask back up and drained the warm contents. He pulled his phone from his pocket, opened the camera app, and hit record.

-5-

I'm a little drunk right now and I haven't slept in days, so I'll try to keep this fairly short. I'm going to recall the dog park incident. Strap in.

When Nolan was four, we lived about an hour from the Bluff Creek Dog Park. Sure there were other dog parks much closer to our house, that didn't involve getting anywhere close to the 405, but it was near the Ballona Wetlands Reserve where Nolan liked to watch the sailboats drift by.

He was a good kid, but hardheaded like his mother, who was long gone by that point. I didn't have the heart to tell him it was ultimately his *condition* which drove her away. Though there weren't many incidents since the day of his birth, she couldn't face the very thing she helped create. She had an image to uphold, a career that wouldn't allow *abnormalities* like their son to be grinning with them in red carpet photographs. Her work continued to slip. Her agent stopped calling. Casting agents quickly forgot. And, much like her career, she slipped away without a word. It was little consolation to Nolan, but a puppy temporarily did the trick.

For the first few years of Nolan's life, I was absolutely terrified to take him out into public. Once we figured out what the problem was, I quickly made him a pair of goggles from my effects studio at home. They were created with the intention of a one-way mirror, reciprocal glass, where Nolan could see everything beyond, but no one could see his eyes. It was difficult explaining to complete strangers why my son wore them every time we stepped out of the house. I taught Nolan to ignore them and to be himself.

Anyway, we went to the dog park. Dutch, our one-year-old golden lab, was thrilled for the day out. As was Nolan. It was a gorgeous day, like most Southern California days in the early summer. It was a Saturday, and after ten minutes of circling, I found an empty spot and parked. Dutch couldn't wait to get out. He was so excited the moment other dogs came into his view. I figured Nolan was big enough to hold his leash until they could get through the gate into the park, so I gave him the handle. I reached back and cracked open the back door after unlocking Nolan from his car seat. My biggest mistake. Dutch nudged open the door and leapt from the car. The cord pulled tight, and Nolan was thrown from the car onto the dusty, gravel covered parking lot. I panicked and rushed around to the other side of the car. My heart stopped.

Nolan's goggles had come off his head.

Quickly, I dove for them, but Dutch was quicker. The lab snatched the goggles in his mouth and took off. I fell and slid on the gravel, opening up the skin on my knees. When I opened my eyes from the pain, an older woman had already opened the gate for the dog. Behind him, my goggle-less son was giving chase.

I stumbled to my feet and chased after them both, screaming for him to get back to the car. By the time I had gotten through the gate, Nolan was nearing a group of women and their dogs under the shade of Mexican fan palms at the back of the park. Dutch dropped the goggles and bounded around the other dogs, while the three other women watched Nolan approach. I yelled with everything I had, cried for them all to cover their eyes. The women stared at me in confusion. The other dogs turned to me in their play, then locked onto Nolan, as he came to a stop before them.

Breathless, I grabbed Nolan from behind and pressed his face into my chest, careful not to look him in the face. I was lucky. The others weren't. I turned back to the women and the dogs, including our Dutch, and they were all staring at Nolan quietly, eyes wide and jaws slack. Even the dogs appeared confused.

Then they all started screaming.

While the dogs hopped around, barking and thrashing their heads, the three women had their own ways of dealing with their pain. One woman, a blonde in her mid-sixties, screamed and pounded her fists against her temples. She turned to the nearest palm tree and repeatedly smashed her skull against its thick trunk. A younger brunette with a short bob, ran to the nearest chain-link fence and dragged her eyes across the spires on the top. Blood spilled down the polished chrome. The other woman, a heavyset African-American, had fallen over and was rolling around the neatly cut grass in a fit. She smashed her head into the ground and pulled at her lips, stretching her skin as far as it would go. One of the dogs had run away, but a beagle had found a small retaining wall where it repeatedly knocked its tiny head against the bricks. The rest of the park visitors raced to us, yelling various obscenities, and did their best to keep the women from harming themselves any further.

While I kept my crying son away from the crowd, I looked around for Dutch. I saw other dogs milling about by themselves, but our dog was nowhere to be seen. Then I spotted him. Somehow he had leapt over the fence and had fled into the parking lot. I could hear him howling—a long, pitiful cry that broke my heart. The dog thrashed its head, unable to cope with the madness spreading through his vulnerable brain.

A blue mini-van came around the corner.

Dutch saw this and lowered himself in front of the oncoming tire.

-6-

It was wrong. It was all wrong.

Daylight had yet to crest over the San Fernando Valley, and Martin was already sweating up a storm. Back and forth he stumbled drunkenly around the set piece his effects team had created. It was the final scene of the film, and though they were days—if not another week or more—away from actually wrapping up production, he was finally ready to say action on one of the film's most crucial moments. He had been waiting forever to shoot this scene. His crew knew how important this was for the wrap-up of the series. And yet all their fuck-ups seemed to shine right at him.

The set was supposed to be a burned-up hospital, the very place the killer was born in the original film, and the room was supposed to be littered with freshly mutilated corpses from the killer's rampage. But everything was wrong. The burnt and mutilated corpses were shoddy, at best. They looked like someone had raided a Halloween store clearance section and tried to cover it up with thin layers of latex stippling. He couldn't understand what he was seeing. They had spent months life-casting and sculpting hyper-realistic corpse dummies for this scene, but they were nowhere to be found. Even the blood looked amateur and far too intentional. There was an art to creating realistic blood splatter, and this looked like a child had finger-painted it. How could he let this happen? He had worked so closely with his crew, had trusted them to not need him nitpicking their every step. He was already under the microscope with the studio and producers, and the investors were on the brink of splitting from the film altogether. He wanted to collapse. This was going to set them back another day, maybe two.

A door banged open from somewhere near the rear of the warehouse, and Martin turned to a red-faced Andrew jogging up to him. Behind Andrew was Floyd Golden, his executive producer. Martin rarely saw Floyd on set. The clean-shaven, slick-haired prick tended to stay out of Martin's way, and Martin was perfectly happy with that. He had only worked with Golden a few times in his career, but rarely was it ever pleasant. He was only on the film because the studio gave Martin no choice.

"Goddamn it, Marty!" Andrew screamed. "Why aren't you answering your phone?"

"I left it in the office. What's wrong?"

Fat tears dripped down Andrew's face. "She's dead, man! She's fucking dead!"

Martin went cold. "*What?* Who's dead?"

"Vanessa," Floyd said calmly.

"*Vanessa* Vanessa? Our Vanessa?"

Floyd nodded.

Andrew cried. "She and some of the cast were partying last night in Malibu. She left drunk and tried to drive home. She swerved and hit a tractor trailer head-on."

"Dear Lord…" Martin's knees felt weak. He grabbed Andrew's shoulder for support. He had been working with Vanessa since film one. Though they fought occasionally on set, Martin loved her like a daughter. His heart broke.

Andrew pulled Martin close and wept into his chest.

Behind him, Floyd Golden watched them both with little more than a sneer. He pulled out his phone and started to dial. He spoke to Martin without looking at him. "I'm shutting down production for the time being. I'm going to have to make some phone calls to find out what we're going to do. Meanwhile, why don't you go sober up, Martin? You look like shit."

Martin broke from Andrew. "Excuse me?"

Floyd continued to play on his phone. "You heard me. We've already wasted enough time on this production with your delays and your drunkenness and shoddy makeup effects. And if this half-assed set is any indication of your continued work on the film, then we're going to be in a lot of trouble. Vanessa Federko's death is a tragedy, but I can't let it derail this film any more than it already is."

Gritting his teeth, Martin growled, "You son a bitch!"

Floyd turned and walked away. "Call me any name you'd like, Wiger, but I'm in charge of this production from here on out. Now if you'll excuse me, I've got a grieving family to attend to. Maybe, if you're not too inebriated, you can join us."

-7-

I'm very tired, and after spending the entire day at a funeral for a good friend and co-worker, this is the last fucking thing I want to do. I've seen enough death in my life, both real and make believe, but I can't help to feel this is all my fault. I've felt responsible for so much death in this world, even though none of it was by my own hand. I mean, Charles Manson is called a killer and not once did he actually murder anyone. Much like Manson's flock, Nolan Wiger was my creation. I don't know why my son has his eyes. Gloria and I were normal people—good people. We only wanted a healthy child.

What we got was pure madness.

It was three years ago, and I was going over footage in the living room from the film I was effects supervising on—Nolan fast asleep on the couch beside me. He hated sleeping alone, and even though I bought him a nice *big boy bed*, he insisted on sleeping with me. I knew I should have broken that habit much sooner, but to be honest, I liked having him near. There was a knock at the door—a loud, insistent strike only a cop could make. I slowly stood up and approached the door.

Before I could speak, I heard, "Mr. Martin Wiger! Open up! We have a warrant!"

I froze, unsure of what to do. In the space of a blink, I ran through every incident I had ever had with the law, but nothing came to mind for why they would need a warrant. I approached the door and unlocked the latches. I had barely begun to turn the doorknob when it was pushed in at me and four officers rushed in with their guns drawn. I threw my hands up and winced.

"What the fuck is this about?" I yelled.

Behind them, two detectives in flat-ironed suits stepped into the house and flashed their badges. The bigger of the two said, "Martin, I presume? We have a warrant for the arrest of a one Mr. Wiger."

Shaking, I said, "Jesus Christ, what did I do?"

The other detective said, "No, not you. The other Mr. Wiger. Nolan Michael."

"Daddy?"

I turned toward Nolan, who had now joined them in the foyer. The officers shifted toward my son and aimed their weapons at him. Two of them rushed him, while the other two shoved me against the wall.

"Hey! Hey! Leave him alone, Goddamn you! What is this about?"

Nolan cried and screamed as he was taken outside.

The tall detective said, "Mr. Wiger, your son is under arrest for the murder of fifteen people."

For a moment I chewed my lip. I ran through my head how many incidents Nolan had had since he was born. I knew of an unfortunate many, but *fifteen*? Were there more I didn't know about? I tried not to let it show. Instead, I raised my voice. "This is ridiculous! You can't do this! He's just a kid!"

"We can and we will, and if you'd like to be taken in right along with him, I suggest you keep it up."

I followed them outside to a driveway teeming with activity. Police cars lined the street, throwing red and blue hues across the faces of my on-looking neighbors. I was already scared out of my wits, terrified of what they were going to do to my child, and the last thing I needed was well-off rubberneckers contacting the media for first rights. The two detectives kept me at bay, despite my trying to push through them, while two other officers led Nolan to a Child Protective Services cruiser parked behind my SUV. I saw one of the cops smack the back of Nolan's head, right at the clasp of his goggles. I screamed and lunged. The two officers laughed and ripped the goggles off his head.

There was nothing I could do. They'd sealed their fate. I screamed for Nolan to close his eyes, but it was too late. Before the cops could push him into the car, they both began to scream. They dropped to their knees, holding their heads, and writhed in agony on my drive-way. Nolan replaced his black-mirrored goggles and stepped away to the back of the cruiser, where he ducked down, crying, with his head between his legs.

The detectives continued to hold me back, while several other officers attempted to help their peers. One of the men rubbed his face against the concrete. The other repeatedly smashed his head with the car door. His face a raw, scraped up mess, the first officer pulled the mace tube from his belt and sprayed its hot contents in his own eyes. Following suit, the other dropped on his back and pulled the pistol from his belt. Before anyone could stop him, he placed the gun against his cheek and fired.

The media wasn't the only one with a story that night.

-8-

"You're being replaced."

The chair under Martin creaked as he leaned forward in shock. "What?"

The group of well-manicured men and women sitting at the long table before him appeared ready for an outburst. Unlike him, they seemed comfortable, if not a bit bored by being there. Martin could tell their hands were twitching for their phones.

Floyd Golden sighed and continued. "Martin, I'm not in the mood to run circles with you. We're all very busy trying to keep this production afloat right now. I think you owe it to me, as well as your producers and investors, to step down. *Gracefully*."

Martin's eye twitched, as if he'd had too much caffeine. "What the fuck are you talking about, step down? This is my movie—*my* movie. I created this entire Goddamn series!"

"And we thank you for all the years of...*entertainment*. But you have to realize this production cannot, and will not, continue under your direction."

"Says who?"

Golden presented his fellow suits with a raised eyebrow. "These well-meaning individuals before you.

And the studio head, Clive Kelly. He wanted to be here, but he is at his son's bar mitzvah in Garden Grove. He did forward this letter." He pushed a piece of paper across the table.

Martin didn't have to read it. He knew what it was, what it demanded. It wasn't his first time seeing an unruly director, but it was definitely his first time receiving one. "This is absolute bullshit, Floyd. Absolute bullshit!"

"No. What's absolute bullshit is the fact we've allowed this production to continue with *you* at the helm. We're now well over a week behind schedule because of your ineptitude. The lovely people before you have lost countless millions because of your late nights, your drinking, and your inability to multitask. And our leading lady is now deceased. You've backed us all into a corner, Martin."

Martin balled his fists. "Are you blaming me for Vanessa's death? That was an accident!"

"An accident, yes, but it never should have happened in the first place. Had we wrapped when we were supposed to, this most likely wouldn't have happened. We should have been done by now."

A shiver ran down Martin's spine. He hated the man more than anything right then. He wanted to leap across the table and slap his perfectly shaved face, but he was right. He would never say it out loud, never give them the satisfaction.

God, I need a drink.

After a few moments of silence, Martin sighed, "So what now? I'm being fired, I take it?"

Golden shook his head. "Not outright, no. But you're being replaced behind the camera. You'll still be in charge of your effects crew—they very obviously need your guidance. Your name will still be credited as creator and writer."

A woman at the end of the table spoke up. "I have some questions about the script. Does there have to be so much *blood* and *death*? It seems so...*excessive*."

Martin sneered. "Script revisions? Really? Right now, this late in?"

Golden interrupted, "Yes, really. We and the new director have some ideas to not only make this a better film, but how to get it back on track and moving forward."

His chair groaned again when he sat back. Martin crossed his arms as he slumped. "Un-fucking-believable. And who, pray tell, is replacing me on *my* movie?"

"Dick Bianconi."

The name was so familiar, but Martin couldn't place it. Then it hit him. "The *porn* director, Dick Bianconi?"

"He's moved on from the adult film industry and is looking to make the jump to mainstream. We've spoken to him extensively over the last few days and we feel he's the right man for the job."

"You can't be serious. I've met the guy. He's a loose cannon. He's known for berating and beating his cast and crew. He's a fucking psycho."

"But a very capable psycho."

Martin spun around just in time to see all six-foot-four inches of Dick Bianconi walk into the room. His Pig-Pen cloud of arrogance followed. Martin had only had a few run-ins with Bianconi, mostly at parties, but the man had never failed to leave a negative impression. Already a failure in Hollywood, he had found his money in the San Fernando Valley porn scene, where his stink always rode back down with the Santa Anna winds. Bianconi had desperately wanted to work with Martin for years and, until now, Martin had been successful in avoiding him.

Bianconi stuck out his hand. "The great Martin Wiger." When Martin didn't reciprocate, Dick pulled is hand back and raised both in a gesture of surrender. "Floyd's right, Martin. We've been discussing ways to get this movie going in the right direction. Look, I get it. This is your baby, and you couldn't get the job done, but I'm here to grab this film's cock and guide it right back in the smooth pussy of success."

Martin rolled his eyes so hard it hurt. "Real classy." He turned to Golden. "You know what? This is all fine and dandy, but you're forgetting one little thing. We have no lead actress, assholes."

Bianconi held a finger up. "*Au contraire, mon frere.* Already way ahead of you. Hon, could you come in here, please?"

The office door creaked open, and the past stepped right in.

She was almost unrecognizable. She no longer carried herself as the Hollywood starlet he'd once known, once loved. She appeared twenty pounds lighter, but most of that lost weight had been repositioned to her new, ample chest. Her once long, beautiful hair was now in a close-cropped pixie cut, and though it didn't look bad, it just wasn't her. Ten years and Martin barely recognized his own ex-wife.

He turned back to his producer. "What the fuck is *she* doing here?"

"Nice to see you, too, Martin," Gloria sighed.

"She," Golden answered, "is the best actress we could get at such short notice. She was quite the up-and-comer years ago, you know?"

"Oh, I'm aware. I'm very aware. I'm also aware she's been doing a lot cumming on screen these days. Or, at least *acting* like it. Isn't that right?"

"Martin!" Gloria said.

Martin screamed, "This is absolute and utter bullshit! What are you assholes trying to pull on me? She doesn't even *look* like Vanessa. You can't just throw her in there and pretend she's the same character! They tried that shit with Heath Ledger in that Doctor Parnassus movie and it didn't work!"

"Dick here will figure it all out in post." Golden stood up and buttoned his jacket. "This is all non-negotiable, Martin. Unless you want to give up all your rights to this film and not get paid, I suggest you shut the hell up and get back to creating fake blood and body parts, and stay out of Dick's way. This is his production now. He's in charge."

His face red hot, Martin bit his tongue until he tasted blood. He gave every face at the table a long, hard look, burning their blank, disinterested stares into his brain, then stood and walked out of the office.

-9-

Martin was rarely in fear of being recognized in public. He wasn't a handsome man, at least not by Los

Angeles standards, which was why he preferred to be behind the scenes. The actors and socialites could have their nightclubs and their paparazzi. Martin would keep his relative anonymity. Which was why he frequented Spicoli's, the watering hole up the street from his Chinatown apartment. The owners knew him, the place was rarely packed, and if he was too drunk to drive, it was only a short walk home. And tonight, drunk was exactly what he was shooting for.

Hours after his meeting, Martin's hands still shook in anger. The bartender, a young woman named Carmen who barely looked old enough to drink, kept a raised eyebrow trained on him as she handed him another Modelo. "Anything you want to talk about, Marty?" she asked.

He shrugged. "You ever had life stick it in and break it off? I mean really stick it in deep?"

"Being a woman in America? Yeah, I'd say I have."

"Touché."

"Can I get you anything else?"

Martin looked up at her and grinned stupidly. "Access to a time machine? Maybe a little more hair on my head? I guess I would settle for your number."

Carmen smiled. "Sure. It's 867-5309."

"Wait—*you're* Jenny? *The* Jenny?"

"Only call for a good time." Carmen winked and stepped away.

"A little young for you, isn't she?"

Her voice sliced into him like razor blades, and he sat up as he turned to her. "What are you doing here, Gloria? Or whatever it is you're going by nowadays. Mary or something?"

Gloria sat her white Michael Kors purse on the bar top before taking the stool next to him. "Marla. Marla Mouth. And I knew you'd be here. This is your place."

Martin snickered. "Marla *Mouth*. Very nice. I'm sure that mouth has been plenty busy over the last seven or so years. How many fuck films have you made now?"

She pulled a vape pen from her purse and took a drag. "I'm not doing that anymore." She rubbed her nose.

"Oh, yeah? What, are you doing those private chatroom sites for money now? Or are you just sucking dicks on the street for the taste of it?"

She didn't seem phased by his insults. "I'm going straight, Marty. I'm getting back to real acting again. I'm not doing those things on film anymore."

He didn't want to look at her, her presence was already enough to make him seethe, but he turned to look her in her eyes anyway. So much had changed in the last several years. Not only had her long hair gone by the wayside, but her other features seemed off. Her eyes were darker and deep set, her nose now thinner and upturned. Her lips were full of collagen, giving them a full, thick pout he didn't remember her having when they were together. Had he not known who she was, he would have never recognized her.

"I can see why they call you Mouth," he finally said. "What do you want, Gloria?"

"I want to talk and make amends. If we're going to be working together, then I want us to get along." She sniffled and scratched at the tip of her nose.

Martin nearly choked on his beer. Suds dribbled down his chin. "Get along? Are you fucking kidding me? Gloria, I was fired from my directing job today and replaced by some half-wit, dime store porn director who probably couldn't properly light a money shot, much less run an actual multi-million dollar production. My passion project is being taken from me and it's going to become utterly unrecognizable. I'm sure most of the cast and crew hate me now because I'm an alcoholic. And then my porn star ex-wife just waltzed back into my life unannounced and says 'Hey! I'm the lead of your movie now, ex-husband who I dipped out on years ago!'"

Gloria rolled her eyes. "Believe it or not, I've gone completely straight. I haven't shot an adult scene in nearly six months. Hell, I haven't even had sex in three."

"Oh? You're a nun now?"

"Christ, Marty, you're giving me a headache. What do I have to do to get a drink around here?"

Martin motioned to the bartender. "Hey, Carmen? Another Modelo for me, and a glass of your finest belladonna for the classy lady here."

"I'll take a Modelo, as well," Gloria said.

Shaking, Martin dropped his head. "I can't believe this is happening."

"We've all got problems. It's how you choose to deal with them that matters. Me? I'm taking my life back into my own hands."

Carmen sat their drinks down and walked away.

"Really? Like the 'running out of coke' kind of problems?"

Gloria narrowed her eyes. "Excuse me?"

Martin sat up. "Don't give me that shit. I know what a coke user looks like. I've been around them all my life. You haven't stopped rubbing your nose since you sat down."

Pulling her hand away from her face, she took a long drink of her golden pilsner. "I've quit."

"It's hard to believe anything you say anymore."

"Well, that's your problem."

Fuming, Martin turned to face her. Noticing the few wandering eyes of the other patrons, he kept himself at a low growl. "You know what my problem is, Gloria? My problem is you have yet to mention our son. You *do* remember we have a child, right? Because *I* haven't forgotten."

She wouldn't meet his eyes. "I'm aware of him, yes."

"*Aware?* Do you not remember the night he was born? I sure as shit remember. I remember how happy we were. I remember how much I loved you and our son."

"I remember the blood. And the screaming."

Martin paused. "Yeah…that was there, too. But despite that, you gave birth to our child. You can't just run out and wait almost a decade to wander back in like it didn't happen. You can love me and leave me, fine, but Nolan is your son. Forever. Despite his ailment."

"Is that what we're calling it these days," she asked, sarcastically. "An *ailment*?"

"You can't keep running away, Gloria. I know you're scared. Hell, I love the goddamn kid more than anything in the whole world, but I'm scared, too."

She swallowed. "You don't know shit."

"What's that supposed to mean?"

Her eyes burned with tears when they met his. "I've seen what he's capable of. Even when you weren't around, I've seen the things he's made people do to themselves." When Martin didn't ask, she said, "I've seen him kill others with his eyes. Many others. Maybe not on purpose, but I've seen it happen. Maybe a dozen times. It…it was horrible."

Martin nodded, regarding the number. "Yes, I'm aware of that number now. It's why he's locked away like an animal at the state hospital with all the other nutcases. Speaking of which…why haven't you visited him?"

Gloria's face twisted into disgust. "Why would I?"

"Because he needs his mother, goddamn it! Because he needs to remember what your face looks like. Your love. He needs to know you care about him and you'll be there for him."

She shook her head and wiped her cheek. "I can't."

Martin scooted his stool closer to her. "You know they're moving him? In about…" He waved his hand over his cell phone's screen so the time and date flashed across. "…eight days they're transferring him to a fully maximum security facility where we'll never be able to see him again. There's not a damn thing I can do about it. I can't file for an extension or a halt in the move because they have ruled him too dangerous to be kept locally. Gloria…we're never going to see our baby again. Don't you care?" Now it was his turn to cry.

Puffing her vape pen, she stood up and grabbed her purse. "I've got to go."

"Excuse me?" he yelled.

"I've got a long day on set tomorrow, so I better get home and get some sleep." She took a handful of ones from her purse and dropped them near her unfinished drink.

Martin shook his head. "You heartless bitch. You truly don't care, do you? You're going to let him be whisked away, out of our lives for good. You're not even going to fight for him?"

Gloria surprised Martin by slamming her fist on the wooden bar top. "Don't you *dare* speak to me that way!" she growled. "You act like you're all innocent in this matter. I know what you've seen him do since I've been away. I've seen it on the news. Even though I've tried my hardest to keep it out of my life, I'm well aware of all of it. You're just as responsible for bringing this—this *murderer* into the world. You're not innocent. If anything you've been exploiting his *affliction* for millions to see. *The Eyes of Madness?* How much money have you made from our child?"

Martin stood up to eye level. "I started those movies before he was born!"

She pushed him back down into his chair. "Sure, but your villain went from blinding his victims to killing people just by looking at them."

He stared at her, unsure of what to say. He thought about it, and a little piece of him crumpled into ash. He never realized what he had done. To him it was the logical next step in the series, the ongoing development to keep the series fresh and exciting. He had no idea he was pilfering from his own life. He wanted to die.

Gloria pulled her purse over her shoulder and scratched at her nose. "Here's where we're going to go from here, Martin. You and I? We're going to strictly be co-workers. Unless you're working directly with me, you're not to speak to me. You're not to get anywhere near me unless it's absolutely necessary. I want to get through this production in one piece, I want to get paid, and I want to never see you again after Dick yells *That's a wrap*. Understood?"

Martin glared at his ex-wife. He said, "Just say his name."

Gloria stared at him as if he were a complete stranger.

"Just say his Goddamn name," he repeated. "Just once."

And like a stranger, she left him to finish his drink alone.

-10-

"Martin?"

The polished leather was warm in his calloused hands. Its curves and edges, all created by him, felt good and right. His hands ached, but his brain chugged along up the hill, urging him to never stop.

"Hey, Martin?"

He gripped the ten-inch industrial filing stick and vigorously rubbed the edge of the eye hole. The mask had to look aged and decayed—much more worn than the one that was thrown into his face earlier by Bianconi. It had to look *older*, the man said.

"Martin?"

So it wasn't good enough? *Fine.* The mask wasn't scary enough? *Fine.* He would work until his mother fucking fingers broke off if it would make everyone happy. Because what did it matter to him? He only created the fucking monster. He only designed the mask well over a decade ago. He only knew what the fuck he was doing! And yet, everyone seemed to know better than him.

"Yo! Earth to Martin! Come in, Martin?"

They didn't know shit. They were still pissing their Goddamn beds and eating their snot when he was on top of the world. He was still Martin fucking Wiger. Forty-nine years old or not, he still deserved better than this.

He would show them better.

A hand clasped his shoulder. Martin whipped around and jabbed the file at the hand's owner. The youngest of his crew, Mike, threw his hands up in defense. "Whoa, man! I didn't mean to scare you!"

Sweat dripping down his face, Martin asked, "What do you want, Lombardo?"

Mike stepped back, looking flustered. "Dick's calling for you on set. He wants to know if the new rendering of the mask is ready. They want to start rolling in fifteen."

Heart thumping, Martin sneered. He eyed the thick leather mask in his grip. Was it ready? Was it up to par with Bianconi's standards, no matter what its creator thought? He was going to find out. Martin dropped the file on the tiled floor and let it clatter under his work bench. Busy working on their own projects, Lisa, Ted, and Marlo all turned to look at him. "Is it ready? Does it fucking look like it's ready, Lombardo? Does it look up to snuff to you?"

Mike looked at him confused. "I guess…?"

Martin screamed, "You *guess*? Is that what I taught you to do—to *guess*? You're supposed to *know*, Lombardo. Guessing is for fucking amateurs! Jesus titty-fucking Christ! Have any of you people ever listened to a word I've said?"

Mike was trembling and looked as if he were going to cry.

"Suck it up, Lombardo, or I'm going to send you back to rural Pennsylvania to make shitty home movies again. Got it?"

The younger man nodded. "What about Dick?"

The leather mask creaked as he squeezed it. "Well, then…let's go see what Dick Bianconi has to say because, hey, it's his final word, ain't it?" Martin stomped out of the lab.

The cast and crew milled about the abandoned boiler room set when Martin entered. Bianconi had his back turned and was speaking to Gloria and the script supervisor when Martin chucked the mask at his back. Bianconi quickly spun around to face him. "What the *fuck* was all that about?"

"Here's the perfect mask you ordered, captain."

Everyone on the stage went silent.

Bianconi eyed him with a bit of humor. "Is there a problem, Marty?"

Martin took few steps toward the bigger man. "First of all, it's Martin Wiger. I've got more clout in my ass hair than you'll ever have in this industry. So don't ever call me *Marty* again. Got it, *Dick*? Second, I will take however long I feel like taking on my work, because I don't fuck my work up in the first place. I've got plenty of awards on my shelves to back me up. And, finally, you will not chastise me in front of these people like I'm some third-rate Halloween prop maker. You may have taken my job behind the camera but this is still *my* movie. *My* creation. Anything going to be changed will have to go through me first. Got it, *Dick*?"

A big smile broke across Bianconi's face. He crossed his arms. "Is that so?"

Martin moved another step closer. "I believe I can't say it any clearer."

"Well, then. Should we go talk to the producers then? Because the last time I checked *I was in charge! And what I say goes!*" Behind him, Gloria flinched at his raised voice. "You're just the fucking special effects guy, you and your group of halfwits. If I want to use CGI'd blood instead of squibs, then that's what I'll do, you arrogant prick. It's my job to get this movie made. That's the reason *you* don't control shit around here anymore! Now…pick up that mask and hand it to me like a gentleman, *Marty*."

Another step, and Martin's fists were balled. "Stick the mask up your pretentious ass."

Bianconi sighed. "Is this really the hill you want to die on?" When Martin didn't answer, he stepped up close enough to whisper in his ear. "You're really embarrassing me in front of my girl, Marty."

Martin glared at him.

"Oh…Gloria and I? We go way back. We have such…amazing chemistry, her and I." He smiled. "Did she squeak when you made her cum, or is that one of my talents?"

Rage took Martin over, and he reared back and slammed his forehead into Bianconi's nose. The bigger man yelped and threw himself sideways, and before Martin could begin to do everything his body urged him to do, two sets of arms from his co-workers dragged him away.

The crew scuttled toward Bianconi to see if he was ok, and gave Martin cold scowls as he was taken away.

-11-

"That's it. You're done."

Martin watched Golden pace back and forth in his tiny office. The room was already cramped, with Gloria and Bianconi standing by watching. Bianconi held a rag to his bloody nose, and Martin wished he had aimed for the man's mouth instead. He would gladly take a few stitches to his cranium if it meant that scumbag couldn't smile for a while.

Martin gripped the edge of the desk and squeezed. "You can't fire me."

Floyd Golden stopped his pacing. "Excuse me? And why the hell can't I?"

"Because I'll sue you for wrongful termination. We have a contract keeping me here on set, whether you like it or not."

Golden scratched his chin. "Hmmm. I also seem to remember everyone signing a clause in their contracts that prohibits acts of violence while under the studio's and my supervision. Or did your memory disappear with the head-butt you delivered?"

"Oh, no. I remember. I remember lots of things. I remember helping get you your first job. I remember, even though I despise you, introducing you to your third wife while you were still with wife number two. I remember being responsible for lining your greedy fucking pockets with money because of my success. No, Floyd, I might be getting old, but an elephant never forgets."

Golden appeared unimpressed with his spiel. "Regardless of our past, this is where I draw the line. I cannot—and *will not*—have you going around attacking your co-workers, you belligerent idiot. I have the safety of my employees and the best interests of the studio and our investors to keep in mind."

"Fuck the investors, fuck the studio, and fuck you, you Patrick Bateman-looking mother fucker!" Martin screamed. "I'm not a threat to anyone except you and that half-wit smut peddler you brought in to steal my movie from me."

Gloria spoke up. "I feel threatened."

Wide-eyed, Martin turned toward his ex-wife. "Excuse me?"

She stepped out from behind Bianconi with a bit of poise in her shoulders. "I don't feel safe when you're around."

Martin stared at her and felt his jaw drop.

"I don't like the way he talks to me," she continued. "And the way he treats others. He comes to work every day drunk and high—you can smell it on him."

"*High?*" he screamed. "*I'm* the high one?"

"Either he goes or I go, Floyd."

Martin pulled at what little hair he had left on his head. "Am I going fucking crazy? What is the matter with you people? You can't do this to me! This is my movie! My series!" *My world*, he thought.

"As of right now, it's not," Golden said, disgusted. "You're officially fired from this production."

Knees weak, Martin kept his white knuckles on the desktop. "You can't…"

"I'll be keeping your team around in your absence, just in case, even though they're proving to be about as worthless as you. They can hang up green screen when we need them."

"No…"

"Pack up what you have in your office and leave the premises immediately. I'm calling security to escort you out."

Martin waved his hand. "Don't bother. I'm…I'm leaving." He turned and pushed past Gloria and Bianconi to step outside.

"Leave your security badge at the front desk," said Golden.

Bianconi leaned in and whispered, "Be seeing yah, champ."

Martin slammed the door behind him.

He brushed past the awkward silence and stares from his former employees. After quickly packing what he didn't want to leave behind into his overnight duffle bag, he plodded outside toward his car.

A black Dodge Charger sped into the parking lot and came to a stop next to his Fusion. Andrew quickly exited the car. "Martin! Only just heard. What the hell happened?"

Martin grabbed the man by the shirt collar and pulled him close. "Where the fuck were *you* when I needed you, Andrew?"

Andrew threw his hands up in defense. "I was getting lunch at Poquito Màs, because I didn't want pizza today. What did you do, man?"

"I got fired from my own movie!" He slowly let Andrew go.

"What? No. Oh, man…Marty…I don't know what to say."

Martin opened his car door and sat inside.

"Is there anything I can do, Marty? I really don't want to leave it like this."

Martin stared straight ahead, the late afternoon sunlight dying behind the tree line. "Just keep your head down, Andrew. And your eyes closed."

-12-

Glass after glass, bottle after bottle, Martin did his best to die of alcohol poisoning. When beer wasn't doing it, he switched to tequila and vodka before finally settling on a heavy glass bottle of Basil Hayden's. Carmen wasn't behind the bar of Spicoli's tonight, and the old hippie server with the Phish bandana tied around his head wasn't going to talk him out of the large tab he was running up. The old man just nodded and kept pouring.

What have I become? Martin drunkenly mused. He used to be on top of the world. He'd had to turn down projects because he simply couldn't split himself into multiples and take on everything he wanted. He'd had a beautiful home in the hills, his dream car, adoring fans, a gorgeous wife...a son. He'd had it all. And much like the noxious mixture sloshing around in his stomach, it was about to be thrown up and flushed down the toilet.

Martin didn't want to be home right now. And though he didn't want company, he wanted background noise. The TV above the bar was showing the Kings and Blues, with ten minutes left in a scoreless hockey game. The only other patron was a middle-aged woman in a St. Louis hat, cheering at every big hit on the screen.

What am I going to do now?

Maybe the effect of his outburst wouldn't be immediate, but it was definitely going to cause a ripple in the system. Martin had seen it before. Actors could get away with yelling and screaming on set, but they were the darlings people paid to see. Anyone behind the camera was expendable. Decades of hard work and sacrifice was about to be gone in a single day. Even though alcohol was a depressant, it was building the rage inside.

Three young men stepped into the bar and ordered themselves a round of Keystones. One of them asked when Rot In Hell was playing, and the bartender told them next Tuesday. The biggest of the three turned and stared at Martin.

After a few moments he said, "You look familiar. You guys, doesn't he look familiar?"

The other two shrugged.

Martin heard them, but continued to stare at the bottom of his glass.

"Yeah," the young man said happily, as the lightbulb went off in his head. "You're Martin Wiger, aren't you? The movie monster guy!"

Martin sighed and shook his head.

The young man took out his phone and typed on his keyboard. "I knew it, man! It is you! I knew I recognized you."

"Who the hell is Martin Wiger?" one of the other two asked.

"Come on, man," he exclaimed. "Martin Wiger is like the Dick Smith of the two thousands."

They looked at their friend in confusion.

"He's like Tom Savini, but better."

"Oh," they said, unimpressed.

The young man turned back to Martin. "I can't believe you're here. I'm such a huge fan. I've seen all your movies. Hell, I dreamed of being just like you when I was a kid." His hands were shaking in excitement.

Martin belched. "Not me."

"What do you mean?"

"I mean…not me. Leave me…alone."

The young man appeared confused. "Could I maybe get an autograph?"

"No."

"Can I least get a selfie with you, Mr. Wiger?

"Please leave me alone," Martin slurred.

The kid quickly stepped up behind Martin and threw an arm over his shoulder. Before he could react, the phone's camera flashed, blinding him. Enraged, Martin swiped the phone from the kid's hand and tossed it across the bar. The device clattered somewhere on the other side of the room. The old hippie and the mom watched him silently.

"Hey, man!" the kid yelled. "What's your fucking problem? That's a five hundred dollar phone, you asshole."

"Bill me," Martin said, and hiccuped.

"You know what, man? You're a prick."

"And you're just some spoiled ankle-biter looking for free shit. Don't you ever get in my face again. You want an autograph or a picture, you little shit? Then buy a ticket at a convention I'm a guest at."

Jesus Christ, Martin thought miserably. *I'm going to be one of those sad fucks who depends on con money to live.*

"Why don't you fellas take it outside," said the bartender.

Martin said, "No need. I—" He didn't finish. A large fist enveloped his view and before he knew it, he was on his ass. He held his nose as bright red blood gushed from his nostrils.

Above him, the three young men glared down. "Sad old fuck," the tall one said. "Can't believe I ever liked this guy." A large wad of warm spit landed right on Martin's forehead.

"Alright," the hippie yelled. "Time to leave! Now!"

The three young men gave Martin one last look before stepping outside. While he rubbed his knuckles, Martin's fan shook his head in disgust and walked away.

Martin lay there for a long time, letting the blood and spit dry on his face. For a moment, he felt alive again.

***

Fifteen minutes later Martin was stumbling back into his apartment, and twenty seconds after that he was vomiting profusely on the tiled kitchen floor, missing the kitchen sink entirely. After miserably heaving the remaining contents out of his stomach, he got up off his knees and threw open the freezer door for something cold to hold against his nose. He could feel it swelling by the minute and imagined the skin around his eyes was darkening—it wasn't the first time he'd taken a punch and become a raccoon for a week.

A small magnetic calendar came loose and fell to the floor. Grabbing a bag of frozen peas, he reached down to pick it up. One particular day stuck out like a lighthouse beacon. Tomorrow's date. Moving day.

Martin stared at it for a long time, unblinking. He let his mind run through rage and empathy, fear and anger—everything that festered in his heart. He dropped the frozen vegetables into the sink and ran into his bedroom for his lockbox.

-13-

The sun hadn't quite peeked over the San Gabriel Mountains, casting the heavy shadow of dawn, as Martin pulled into the parking lot of the hospital. Everything on him shook—hands, chest, teeth—but one thing remained steady. His brain was resolute. And he wouldn't allow that little voice in the back of his head to change his mind. Let the fucker drown in the vodka.

After nearly thirty minutes, an unmarked car pulled out from the fenced-in parking lot on the east side of the building. Martin studied the car closely, and when he counted two and a half occupants inside, he put his Fusion into drive and followed, keeping a safe distance. He began to worry when they led him onto I-605 North rather than taking the exit toward LAX. He pulled out his phone and asked Google for nearby airports. Martin assumed they were heading to the smaller, more private airport thirty minutes north, in El Monte. Satisfied, he gripped the wheel and crept closer to the tan Crown Vic.

They slowed and took the exit for Valley Boulevard. Martin saw his chance and sped up, using the shoulder to pull ahead. He turned abruptly and came to a stop in front of the other car, causing it to slam on the brake to avoid hitting him. He was out of the car before they had time to question his motives. Heart racing, Martin took several strides toward the car, gun pointed directly at the driver.

"Get out of the fucking car!" Martin's gun hand flinched toward the window. "Now!"

Martin heard Nolan yell from inside the car, "Daddy!"

The man behind the wheel fumbled for something on his lap. Martin squeezed the trigger once and a quarter sized hole appeared in the hood of the car. Everyone screamed, the two in the back seat ducking. The man behind the wheel threw his hands up.

Martin yanked the driver's side door open. He recognized the driver immediately—the smart mouthed, crewcut cop from Nolan's hospital room. Growling, Martin told him to unbuckle, then yanked him from the car and pushed him to the asphalt. He stepped over the prone cop and before he could fight back, Martin slammed the butt-end of his pistol into the man's head. He kept going until the man was unconscious. "That's for calling my son a little shit." In the backseat, Dr. Brolan stared, wide-eyed, and continued to hold Martin's crying son down.

Satisfied, Martin stood and popped open the rear door. Dr. Brolan kept a tight grip on Nolan. "You can't do this!" the doctor screamed. "You can't just take him like this! You have no right!"

"I can and I will." He pointed the gun at him. "He's my son, you worthless fuck. You're not going to send him anywhere."

Carefully he helped Nolan exit the car. Martin pulled him close and hugged him tight. The boy continued to cry, shivering as he held onto his father. Tears dripped from Martin's eyes.

"Come on, bud. Stop your crying. You don't want to drown in your goggles, right?" Nolan offered a small giggle, and it felt damn good to hear him laugh again.

"Please," Dr. Brolan pleaded. "Please, just let us take him up north. They may not be able to help him, but they can keep him away from others. How many more have to suffer? How many more lives have to end because—"

"*Because what?*" Martin screamed.

The doctor swallowed hard. "Because of his eyes, Martin. His *Devil Eyes*."

Nolan at his side, Martin crouched down to scowl at the terrified doctor. "Those eyes, Doc? They belong to the only thing I have left in this world—the only good, pure thing. I don't care what he's done in the past or what he'll do ten years from now, as long as he's healthy and happy and he's away from thieves like you who want to study him, or lock him in a cage and toss the key. Today, Doc? Today is the day Wiger's stop taking shit from people who believe they know what's best for us. Today, Doc, *you're* going to be the experiment—"

"No!" the man screamed. He struggled to release his seat belt.

"—and we'll see how long you can withstand the madness."

Martin spun Nolan toward the older man and pulled the goggles up over his forehead. The boy winced at the morning sunlight.

Doctor Brolan kept his eyes clamped shut and whimpered like a scolded child. Martin looked around the highway exit. It was quiet and empty now, but he knew he didn't have a lot of time. He leaned in, moving Nolan closer to the doctor as he did so. Pushing the barrel of the pistol to the doctor's forehead, he demanded, "Open them. Now."

The doctor reluctantly did so. Shaking, the doctor's eyes fluttered open. Unable to escape Nolan's gaze directly in front of him, Brolan's eyes widened. When the doctor's mouth dropped open and he began to scream, Martin pulled Nolan back and replaced the goggles over his eyes before turning the boy around so he couldn't see.

But Martin wanted to watch. As Nolan reached up to cover his ears, Martin kicked the door shut to muffle the noise. Martin didn't need to hear it, he could see the man struggle. Doctor Brolan shrieked and thrashed in the back seat of the unmarked police car. He pulled on his hair, he scratched at his cheeks, pressed his fingers into his eyes. He slammed his head off the front headrest, but quickly turned his attention to the window and repeatedly smashed his skull against the tempered glass. After several strikes, blood sprayed across the glass. When Martin had enough, he smiled and led Nolan back to his car and the two took off.

-14-

Nolan continued to cry in the backseat, and after ten minutes when it didn't stop, Martin pulled the car over to the side of the freeway. His son's pitiful cries made him debate maybe to go back and take care of whatever was left of his doctor himself, but more importantly he was happy his boy was close enough for Martin to hear him at all. He would take any emotion over the lonesome sound of his own tears.

"Nolan? Buddy?"

Keeping his hands over his face, Nolan turned his head toward the window, refusing to look toward Martin.

"Bud, come on. Talk to me."

Nolan said, "Why did you make me do that?"

"Do what?"

"Hurt Dr. Brolan! I-I-I- didn't like that." He began to cry harder.

Heartbroken, Martin unbuckled his seatbelt and climbed into the backseat. He grabbed Nolan and held him against his chest, stroking his soft blond hair. He never thought this was going to happen again, to be able to embrace his child, to be the parent he always wanted to be. He thought his little boy would be gone forever, lost somewhere between a steel fence and a harsh, indifferent world. Martin often stayed drunk to numb his pain, but now, with his child held close, he was as sober as the day Nolan came into this world. Despite the boy's distress, he couldn't have asked for a better moment.

Martin pulled him away and watched his reflection in the boy's black mirrored goggles. "I know you didn't want to do it, bud. I know. But sometimes…sometimes we have to do things we don't want to do. Necessary things. Things that make our lives easier—things that benefit both of us. Dr. Brolan? Bud, he wanted to take you away from me forever. Did you know that?"

Nolan shook his head. "No. He said we were going on an adventure. We were going to fly somewhere fun."

Martin sighed, "Of course he did. Look, bud…you're almost a teenager. Yeah, you're a few years away, but I'm going to talk to you like an adult right now because I think you deserve it. Is that ok? Can we go *mano e mano*?"

The boy nodded.

"Ok, then." Martin bit his lip. "First off, Dr. Brolan was not a very nice man. Nobody in your hospital was very nice. They weren't taking you on *an adventure*, Nolan. They were taking you to another hospital up north, in Washington state, where I would never see you again. I wouldn't be able to visit you or make sure they're treating you the way you should be treated. I couldn't let them break us apart." Now the tears were falling down Martin's face. "I know I haven't been there for you the last few years. I've done everything I could to make us a family again, but if hurting Dr. Brolan was the only way to bring us together, then I'd make you do it again twenty times over. I know you don't want to hurt anyone anymore, but what happened back there? That was one of those necessary things. Do you understand?"

Nolan was quiet for a few moments. He wiped his nose with the back of his hand. "What's wrong with me?"

Martin sadly chuckled. "Other than being *my* son? Not a damn thing. You're perfect the way you are, bud. I wouldn't change a thing."

The boy nodded. "I'm tired."

"I know. Me, too."

"Are we going home?"

Martin took Nolan's hand in his own. "Not yet. We have one more stop to make. Ever wanted to visit a movie set?"

-15-

As they pulled up to the security booth of the small studio lot, Martin made sure to have Nolan sitting on his lap. He drove slowly up to the closed gate and stopped. The security guard, an older man with long white hair pushed behind his ears, stepped out and eyed him.

"Come on, Mr. Wiger," he said, crossing his arms in annoyance. "What are you doing here?"

Martin stared straight ahead. "Open the gate, Charles."

He sighed. "It's too early for this, Mr. Wiger. You know better. You can't come back in, as per Mr. Golden's instructions. Now unless you're dropping off your security badge you neglected to leave behind yesterday, I suggest you turn around and skedaddle before I call the cops."

Now Martin sighed. "Don't make me do it, Charles."

"Excuse me?" The old man looked nervous and reached back into the booth for his phone.

Martin grabbed the top of Nolan's head and, looking away, pulled the boy's goggles up. After a few moments of silence, the old man started to scream and thrash around inside his tiny booth. In a matter of moments all four of the glass windows were splintered and cracked as Charles went from one to the other, smashing his forehead. Blood gushed from his eyes and nose. He pulled at his white locks, tearing them out by the fistful. Grabbing his desk, Charles then drove his head through the plate glass window facing their car. His face was shredded. He ripped two long, jagged pieces of glass free from the sill and jabbed them into his temples.

Martin replaced the goggles, and Nolan slid off his lap to the passenger seat. Martin reached into the booth and opened the gate.

Even though it was just before seven am, the parking lot was full but fortunately devoid of life. Martin found a parking spot and, pistol tucked into the back of his pants, they exited the car, overly cautious of every noise they made. Hand-in-hand, they crept to the side door. Charles had been right, Martin had purposely neglected to turn in his security badge. He pinched the badge in his fingers, hopeful they hadn't wiped it clean from their computer system. They hadn't, and the door softly clicked open for them.

They stepped into the back hallway. The hallway reeked of body odor and old cigarettes and weed, but was free of cast and crew. The coast was clear. Martin eyed a few empty beer bottles sitting underneath the staircase, noting *he* wasn't the only one who was sneaking drinks on set. *Fucking bastards.* Martin gripped Nolan's hand tighter and pulled him along. The boy planted his feet and stopped their progress.

Martin turned with an arched brow. "What's wrong?"

His lower lip jutting out, Nolan began to cry again. "I don't want to do this."

Martin sighed and found his heart shattering all over again. He dropped down to a knee. "Listen, bud. This is something we have to do. Remember when we talked about necessary things? Well, this is a *big* necessary thing. The biggest. Bigger than Thor. Bigger than The Hulk."

"Bigger than Thanos?"

Martin grinned. "Yes, even bigger than intergalactic Grimace. Look, bud, I need you to be strong for Daddy, ok? I know this isn't what you want, but this is something Daddy needs you to be strong for. Can you be a big, strong boy for me?"

Nolan sniffled. "I want to be a man."

"You're only ten. How about we settle for *young* man?"

The boy nodded.

Martin stood. "Whatever happens, bud, I want you to be strong. Show no fear. Make everyone see what an impressive young man you are. You aren't confined to a room anymore, Nolan. There aren't any more doctors or nurses or police to tell you what to do. You're your own person now. You're better than them—all of them. Now, let's go show them who you are."

Nolan cracked a wide smile that Martin knew sparkled in his goggle-covered eyes. It was the first one Martin had seen in so long, and though he wanted to stay and relish it, they had work to do. Together they crept along the dimly lit hallway until they reached the studio doors. The green light above the door signaled it was ok to step on set. Filming had yet to start.

Martin looked down at his son. "Love you, bud."

"You, too, Dad."

With a deep breath, Martin threw the doors open and walked onto the chilled, cavernous set. Before him, the set was teeming with crew workers scurrying about—adjusting the massive tungsten lights, the Director of Photography framing the shot, electrical workers in the background hanging cables out of the way. They stepped closer, and Martin recognized the scene. Even though it wasn't part of the shooting schedule the day before, the final scene of the film was up and ready to be filmed. But it wasn't complete, not by his standards. The set was a burned-out garage, and the floor was supposed to be teeming with bones and smoldering corpses, the final brutal battle between the killer and the heroine, Vanessa's former character, now Gloria's. Instead of the body parts he and his team had made months prior, the floor and walls were covered in layers of bright green screen. More laziness and cost-cutting. Martin gritted his teeth and stepped onto the set with Nolan.

The crew stopped at once and eyed him in silence. Larry, the DP, frowned and stood from his seat. "Martin... What are you doing here?"

Martin asked, "Where is everyone?"

Larry glanced around, confused. "What do you mean? The cast are doing a quick meeting and rehearsal before we shoot."

"And Bianconi?"

The man shrugged. "Either there or in his office. What's this all about, Marty?"

Martin grimaced as his eyes bounced from face to face. "You all gave up on me. This was my movie—my baby—and you all threw me under the bus."

Larry stepped forward with a worried look. The rest of the crew crept closer as well. "Marty...we did no such thing. Your drinking got you fired. Striking a superior got you fired. It sucks, man, but that's life." He glanced down at Nolan. "Is that your son?"

Martin glared at him.

Larry didn't see the anger in Martin's face, as he motioned to the boy. "Why does he have those on?"

Martin stepped behind the boy. "Would you prefer them off?" He lifted the goggles and pulled them free from Nolan's head.

Like a tsunami, a tidal wave of screams and cries washed over them, thick and laborious. The entire soundstage echoed in pain as the crew members struggled with their madness. They grabbed their heads in agony, pulled at the skin of their faces, and dug into their eyes with wild, thrashing fingers.

Tommy, the key grip, ripped the Manfrotto tripod from its taped off spot on the floor and used it to bash in his own skull. Bright red blood ran down his forehead into his eyes and over his lips, spraying the air in a fine mist as he gasped for breath.

Sam, the production's head gaffer, ran straight for one of the Arri lights and threw its barn doors open to reveal the golden blaze beneath. His hands sizzled and blackened at the touch of the scorching metal, and his face immediately blistered being so close to the light. His eyes ruptured from the heat, pouring down his face like pink glue. Instead of dropping dead, he threw himself head-first into the light, and erupted in flames. The other lighting technicians, Tito and Eddie, followed suit and threw themselves into the white-hot fire. The room began to fill with acrid smoke, which burned Martin's eyes and nose.

Patty, from hair and makeup, used a large can of hairspray to blind herself, and when the bottle emptied she put the can in her mouth and attempted to punch it down her own throat. Martin watched as shattered teeth dribbled down her widely stretched lips.

Larry hadn't moved from his position in front of Nolan. He screamed loud and hard, continuing to stare at Martin. He turned and grabbed the clapboard from the director's chair and, taking the skinny upper part in his grip, smashed the long piece of lacquered wood into his eye. There was surprisingly little blood as the man collapsed to his knees.

Beyond Martin and Nolan, several electricians had hung themselves from the low rafters of the set with various ties and cables. A few of them were already dead, but one still jittered at the end of his rope. The man pulled himself up a few inches at a time and released himself with a heavy drop. When he didn't die, he repeated the process.

When the commotion finally died down, Martin replaced Nolan's goggles and led them to his old workstation. The room appeared cold and dark. When he snapped the light on, Lombardo appeared in front of him and plunged a long, serrated knife into Martin's stomach. Martin yelped in surprise.

A look of fearful jubilation washed over Lombardo's face. "I got you, you murdering motherfucker!"

Martin carefully stepped backwards, and the knife slowly extended back out of the hollow hilt, revealing no wound, no blood.

The look of cockiness drained from Lombardo's face, as he realized he had grabbed a retractable blade instead of a real one from the prop case. Martin growled and punched Lombardo square in the nose. The kid fell on his ass, and before Martin would allow him to get back on his feet, he pulled Nolan into the room and flashed him his eyes. Lombardo screamed and covered his face. He rolled on the floor, smacking his skull against the linoleum. He took the industrial file Martin had dropped the day before and pressed it as hard as he could against his forehead. He looked at it then threw it aside, grabbing the spiraled hose of the air compressor tucked under Martin's old desk. Without hesitation, he stabbed the long silver nozzle into his left eye, and squeezed the trigger.

Martin wasn't prepared for the effects. Unlike Larry, this eye provided copious amounts of blood as a plume of fluid blew out of Lombardo's face and splattered across Martin's pants. It bubbled out of his mouth and ran down his ears. What was left of his eye had found a new home on the young man's chin.

Something crashed in the office deeper inside the room. Martin yelled, "Come out. All of you. Now."

The door cracked open, and Marlo, Lisa and Ted gingerly stepped out. They shook in terror, looking from Martin to Lombardo's twitching corpse to the open door behind him.

"What did you do to him, Marty?" Lisa wept.

"The same I'll do to you if you don't shut the fuck up." Martin watched their horrified faces. "Go home. All of you. You're all better than this." He stepped aside and let them scurry out of the room.

He knew they would call the police, if they hadn't already, which didn't leave them a whole lot of time. Nolan was surprisingly quiet. The boy stared at the body of Martin's former protégé without a word or a tear. Martin was very thankful his son was finally understanding their purpose.

With confidence, Martin led Nolan back across the set, littered with the still-smoldering bodies of the crew. *Now* that's *how the actual set is supposed to look.* He snatched a small toolbox from the ground. Nolan's grip in one hand, toolbox in the other, he made his way over to the glass fronted meeting room. The window blinds had been pulled down, and the lights were off. Martin didn't bother with the door handle. He stepped forward and drove his boot into the thin, wooden door. The door splintered as it swung inward, and the cast shrieked as the two of them stepped inside. He let go of Nolan's hand and flicked on the lights. The cast was crowded in the far corner behind the ten-foot reading table. All six-foot-six of Mickey Highmark, the film's villain, shielded them from the oncoming threat, his giant chest bravely puffed out in defiance.

Martin located Andrew in the back and nodded at him. "Andrew. Out. Now."

Andrew swallowed and reluctantly stepped out from the pack. Hands shaking, he walked slowly toward Martin, not meeting his eyes. When he got close enough, Martin grabbed him by the shirt and flung him out of the room. Martin turned back to the actors with a sneer. He tossed the toolbox, and its contents clattered across the tabletop—screwdrivers, hammers, and pliers. Then Martin pulled Nolan in front of him and lifted the boy's goggles. Martin watched as each in turn reacted with widened eyes of their own, or slacked jaws. When they'd all been affected, he quickly guided Nolan from the room.

Andrew cowered before them. "What have you done, Marty? You've gone cra—"

Martin's fist stopped him from finishing. He clocked Andrew across the face, and the smaller man tumbled to the floor, unconscious. Martin made sure he was breathing, which he was, and took Nolan's hand.

"We've got one more stop, bud," Martin said. "You doing ok?"

His son nodded, looking around the set. The small fire illuminated the black glass of his goggles.

"You sure? We can stop this right now if you don't want to continue. I promise."

Nolan looked up to him and smiled. "Let's keep going."

Martin smiled back. "That's my boy."

-16-

They hadn't spotted Bianconi yet, and Gloria wasn't in the meeting room with the other actors. There was only one other place Martin could find them. Down the back hallway, thunderous techno music blared from his old office, the seismic bass only muted by the closed door. Martin told Nolan to stay put and pressed him against the wall. Blood rushing through his ears, Martin slowly clicked open the door and stepped inside.

The music was like a brick wall, guarding Bianconi, Golden, and Gloria from the outside world, and he knew they had not heard anything, knew nothing about what had happened. In the back of the room, Golden and

Bianconi stood side-by-side, both of them naked from the waist down, their pants crumpled at their ankles. Shirtless, her large, fake breasts pulled free over the top of her bra, Gloria was squatting between the two. The men's erect cocks had a neat line of cocaine drawn across them, and Martin watched as Gloria snorted each one before taking their members into her mouth in turn. She switched from cock to cock and even placed both in her mouth at the same time. Both of the men had their heads tilted upward, eyes closed in ecstasy. Bianconi moaned loudly and licked his lips, his nose thick and swollen.

Martin roared. He ripped the pistol from the back of his pants and squeezed the trigger. The cream-colored wall behind Bianconi's head was painted in brains before his lifeless body dropped to the couch behind him. Martin aimed at the stereo and shut that up as well. The momentary silence was shattered as Gloria screamed and shuffled to the wall.

Panicked, Golden yelped and dropped to a squatted protective position, hiding his quickly fading erection. *"What the fuck are you doing?"* he shrieked. He looked at the dead director and gore-soaked wall. His face spasmed with tears. "You…you fucking killed him. You fucking psycho! You killed Dick!"

Martin aimed the gun at Golden. He pulled the trigger, and Golden's groin exploded beneath his shirt. Golden screamed, and Gloria joined him, yet his cries rose much higher in pitch than hers did. He sank lower to the floor, moving from a squat to sitting on the floor as dark blood soaked its way into a rough circle in the thin blue carpet.

"Two dead dicks." Martin couched low in front of him. "I want you to think of one thing for me before I put another bullet into you. Just one thing, Floyd. Can you do that for me?"

Golden shivered on the floor, his face flushing white.

"I want you know you don't own me, Floyd. Not anymore. I'm a free man. My son is a free man, as well. You? Even if I don't kill you, nobody would care. I've got adoring fans all over the world. I will be remembered when I'm dead. Praised for my work. Studied. Idolized. You? You're nothing but a name that quickly flashes across the screen during the opening credits. Nobody—*nobody*—will miss you when you're gone. Unlike me, you're as replaceable as they come. They'll mention you on the news briefly when all this comes out, and just like that—" Martin snapped his fingers, "—gone forever. Open your mouth." He placed the hot barrel of the gun against Golden's pale, quivering lips, and when Golden attempted to fight, he shoved the gun in as far as it could go. Teeth snapped from his gums and tumbled down his throat. Martin emptied the clip into Floyd Golden's head.

He turned to Gloria who was still cowering in the corner of the room. She screamed and cried, tears pouring down her cheeks. "Please don't hurt me! Please! I'm so sorry, Martin."

"Sorry for what, exactly?"

"For everything! For the way I treated you, for lying to get you fired. I'm so…so…so sorry."

Martin dropped the blood-stained gun on the floor in front of her. "That's great, Gloria. Just superb. But I'm not the one you should be apologizing to."

She looked up at him, confused.

"Save your apologies for your son." He walked back to the door, then opened it and guided Nolan into the room.

Gloria immediately began to cry again. She manically threw herself against the far wall, as if she would somehow break through the brick and mortar to escape.

Nolan glanced around the room before settling his gaze on Gloria.

"Do you know who that is?" Martin asked his son.

Nolan shook his head.

"Of course not. She looks a lot different from the last time you saw her. That's your mother, bud."

He stared at her for a long time as she squirmed. She refused to look at him, instead keeping her face buried in her hands. He looked up to Martin and shook his head no.

"Come on, bud. You don't recognize your own mother?"

The boy trained his goggled eyes on her, and for a split second a smile flashed across his lips. "Mommy?"

Martin clapped his shoulder. "That's right. Why don't you go give her a big hug?"

"*No!*" Gloria screamed. "Keep him away from me! Don't let him get near me!"

Nolan's smile faded as fast as it had come. His head dropped and his shoulders slumped, and Martin knew he was going to cry once more. Martin couldn't allow it. He dropped to a knee and whispered, "Buddy, you know what to do."

Turning away, Nolan tried to go for the door. Martin stopped him. "I don't want to," he whined. Nolan's tone pleaded with his father as much as his words did.

Martin squared up the boy's shoulders. "I know you don't. I get it. But think of this, son. Think about all of those lonely nights at the hospital, all those times you wished she was around to hold you and read to you and tuck you in at night. But she didn't want to do any of those things. Not with you, not with me, not with either of us. She was scared of you. She didn't want to love you. That's why she ran away. She didn't want to be your mother. She *hated* you."

Nolan said nothing, only looked at the floor. He breathed in heavily through his nose, his lower lip tucked between his teeth, and for a moment Martin was sure the boy was going to step past him and flee. Instead, the boy spun around and took two strong steps toward his mother, then pulled the goggles up to his forehead.

Gloria screamed and kept her eyes covered.

Martin ran over and, keeping his eyes closed, grabbed Gloria's arms and pulled them away from her face. She thrashed in his grip, clawing at his face with her nails. After a few moments of struggling, he grabbed her under her chin and reached over her head with his other hand to pull open her eye lids.

Then she *really* started to scream. Martin let her go and crawled back behind his son. When the madness finally caught her, Gloria screamed like no one Martin had heard before. He stared at her with awe and pity, the way a zoo visitor watches an animal pace helplessly in a cage. She cried as she clawed at her hair and face, make-up running down her cheeks. She pounded the floor and smashed her face against the carpet. When that offered her no relief, she swiped the pistol from the floor and stuck the bloody barrel into her mouth. She squeezed the trigger but it only offered her a small, dry click, which made her scream harder around the bloodied steel. She tossed the gun aside and maniacally searched for something to hurt herself with. Martin stepped forward and kicked her to the ground when she reached for the cup of pens and pencils on the desk. She screamed in frustration and reached again, but was met with his boot once more.

"*Make it stop!*" she cried.

She tried to root through Bianconi's pants pockets, but Martin grabbed her and threw away from the director's body. He refused to allow her a single thing with which to hurt herself. He wanted her to ride it out, to suffer as he and Nolan had.

Left with nothing but her hands, Gloria began to rake her nails against her cheeks, drawing lines of blood which mixed with her tears. She gouged at her eyes, pushing them further into her head. She tore her teeth into her lips, ripping large chunks from the soft skin Martin used to kiss. She wrenched at the open wounds, and her flesh slowly ripped across her face. She pulled harder, revealing her blood-stained molars beneath. Vomit burst past her lips and through the newly opened holes, adding to the already noxious stench of the room. She tore at her throat with her fake nails that matched her fake breasts. Her body convulsed and spasmed as it started to shut down, but her hands continued to alleviate her pain. When the skin on her cheeks would tear no further, she gripped the flesh around her eyes and yanked with all she had left. Bright white bone met the open air as she dragged the skin and tissue away from her body. She may have been unrecognizable to Nolan, but now she was a complete stranger to Martin, too.

-17-

My entire life was spent searching for the perfect scare. Looking for the perfect way to entertain, while leaving people shocked. I've spent years cultivating my craft, elevating my name, trying to touch the top of the world with my work. But, to be perfectly honest with you, I've never felt whole. I've never felt like I achieved my goal. There was always this little nagging voice in the back of my head that said there was something more out there, that I could do better. Maybe I became complacent or lazy. Hell, I don't know.

I thought *Part Five* would be my magnum opus. *The Eyes of Madness* wasn't a perfect series. It started out as a lazy slasher flick, but it became more. Much more. It evolved into something unique, something special. I evolved, too. I told my crew a few weeks ago this would be my last film. Even though I feel it, I know I'm not that damn old, but I wanted to go out on top. I thought I had created the best scares of my career.

But that wasn't true.

I didn't realize until now I had created my best scare over ten years ago. And while I may never truly never understand him, or what makes him the way he is, he will always be the best thing that ever happened to me. Not my awards or my accolades or my fans. Those fade with time. My little boy? I would die for him.

I've been making these videos for a while now. I thought maybe they were just for me, something so I could reminisce when I was feeling down. At the time my child was gone, and I was all alone. But I'm not alone. He's free.

I'm free.

You're never going to see my last film, and for that I'm sorry. But I will leave you with this. I give to you my last scare. My ultimate fright.

Because fuck you, that's why.

***

Martin shielded his face as his child stared deep into the camera lens of his phone. He waited for twenty seconds, then replaced the boy's goggles. While Nolan rested on the couch, and the police sirens crept closer, Martin quietly uploaded the video to YouTube. Martin winked at the boy. Nolan grinned back.

When he was finished, they left the soundstage together, and hand-in-hand, they welcomed whatever was waiting for them outside.

Story Notes

My favorite band Mastodon has a song on their very first EP *Lifesblood* (or the 2006 reissue *Call of the Mastodon*) called "We Built this Come Death." It's not a great song—or really a very good album to begin with—but there's a sample at the start of the track that's very disturbing. It's a man, whose voice continues to swell in volume and tone, describing experiments being done on men that drove them mad. They would, "*Pull out their hair to relieve the pressure, and tear their heads and faces with their fingers and nails to maim themselves in their madness.*" All of this is being said while a chorus of yells and screams crescendo in the background. Supposedly it was audio taken from the Nuremberg Trials in Nazi Germany, where German soldiers were accused of crimes against humanity, including medical experiments on prisoners of war. It's really unnerving stuff, and it stuck with me for a long time. It ultimately became the first little nugget of this novella idea. Granted, this wasn't originally supposed to be a novella. I had planned on it being a longish short story, but once I had begun to outline it, I quickly realized there was much more there to explore. And maybe…just maybe…there's still more to find out about Martin and his unique offspring.

Just don't go looking for their video online.

Trust me.

ABOUT THE AUTHOR

Wesley Southard is the author of The Betrayed, Closing Costs, One For The Road, and Resisting Madness, and has had short stories appear in outlets such as Cover of Darkness Magazine, Eulogies II: Tales from the Cellar and Clickers Forever: A Tribute to J.F. Gonzalez. When not watching numerous hours of ice hockey, he spends his free time reading and drinking copious amounts of Diet Dr. Pepper. He is also a graduate of the Atlanta Institute of Music, and he currently lives in South Central Pennsylvania with his wife and their cavalcade of animals. Visit him online at www.wesleysouthard.com.

Made in the USA
Middletown, DE
26 January 2021

30911316R00172